Praise *for* ...
Susan Ma...

Someone Like ...

"When you thi... ...ing stories, think S... ...ers a top-notch story."

—*Romantic Times* (4½ stars, Top Pick)

The Marcelli Sisters Trilogy

"This trilogy looks to be a real winner with Mallery's delightful humor, believable characters and an unusual couple...."

—*The Best Reviews* on *The Sparkling One*

"[Susan Mallery] tells an exceptional story with rich characters and a hot love story."

—*Amazon.com* on *The Sassy One*

"Affectionate and emotional... Reading a Susan Mallery book is always a marvelous experience."

—*Romantic Times* on *The Seductive One*

Married for a Month

"*Temptation Island* meets *Oprah* in [this] contemporary romp... [This] sweet story will delight as it provides food for thought."

—*Publishers Weekly*

Sweet Success

"A wonderfully fast-paced delight! You can never go wrong with Ms. Mallery's fascinating storytelling."

—*Romance Reviews Today*

"Witty dialogue, plenty of romantic tension, and delicious characters."

—*Publishers Weekly*

Susan Mallery

Susan Mallery makes her home in Southern California, where the eccentricities of a writer are actually considered normal—what a relief! When she's not busy working on her latest novel, she can be found cruising the local boutiques in her quest for yet another pair of shoes. Susan would love to claim to be a fabulous gourmet chef, but she is not. She does, however, do fabulous take-out ordering and always serves said take-out on lovely china.

THERE'S ALWAYS PLAN B

Susan Mallery

THERE'S ALWAYS PLAN B

isbn 0373880510

This edition published by arrangement with Harlequin Books S.A.

TheNextNovel.com

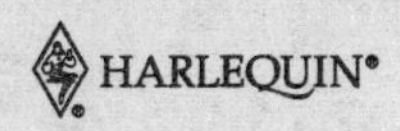

PRINTED IN U.S.A.

To Gail Chasan who said
this would be a great idea,
and who turned out to be right.

CHAPTER 1

"I don't know why you always have to torture me," fifteen-year-old Tiffany Spencer said as she folded her arms over her chest and stared out the passenger-door window. "Some moms actually like their children. Some moms care about their happiness. Why can't you be like that?"

Carly Spencer tightened her grip on the steering wheel and tried to figure out why she'd ever complained about her daughter asking, "Are we there yet?" when she'd been younger. Given a choice between that question and the one currently on the table, "Are we there yet?" seemed amusingly simple to deal with.

"I care about your happiness," she said, even though she knew it was a huge mistake to engage her daughter. At this point it was obvious Tiffany simply wanted to be the martyr to all decisions parental.

"Ha! Oh, sure. Because dragging me away from all my friends and my school and Justin Beakly, who looks just like Matt Damon and who was probably going to ask me to the Spring Carnival dance, is going to make me faint with happiness. Here I am. Fainting."

Tiffany collapsed against the door. Carly hoped her daughter would stay mock-unconscious for at least ten minutes or until the headache remedy Carly had popped a few minutes before had a chance to kick in.

But it was not to be.

"And if we had to leave all that because you're so determined to ruin my life," Tiffany said seconds later, "you could have at least let me get my belly button pierced. I mean what's the big deal? It's *my* body. I bet I'll be the only high school girl here, too, without one. Although maybe not. Have they heard about piercing at the ends of the Earth?"

Her daughter was certainly bright enough, Carly thought, as she desperately searched for a silver lining in what felt like the world's largest dark cloud. Eventually Tiffany would learn to use her highly developed verbal skills for good instead of mother abuse.

"I don't know what they've heard," Carly said cheerfully. "It's possible they're still existing with horse-drawn carriages and cooking on an open fire. Maybe we'll be so modern, they'll think we're aliens from another planet and they can worship us like goddesses."

Tiffany rolled her eyes. "You're not helping."

"Ditto."

"What do you mean by that?"

"You're not helping, either," Carly said. "This move is tough on me, too."

"But it's your fault we have to go." Tiffany sounded outraged. She turned in her seat and glared. "If you hadn't made Dad leave, we wouldn't be doing this."

Carly drew in a deep breath and counted to ten. When that didn't work, she counted to twenty, then promised herself no matter what, she would go to the grocery store later, buy a pint of Ben & Jerry's cookie dough ice cream and eat the entire thing by herself.

Tiffany was a still a child, she reminded herself. Under the carefully curled blond hair, the formfitting clothes and too much makeup lurked a young teenager not yet prepared to deal with the realities of the world.

"Your father and I divorced by mutual decision," she said slowly, going for an "I'm so calm" voice instead of the shrill tone that lurked just beneath the surface. "There were a lot of issues, some of which are private."

"He quit his job." Tiffany sounded both shocked and scared. "Just like that. He says he's sailing to Hawaii."

"I heard that, too." At times she thought her soon-to-be ex was a complete mystery. Other times she hoped he got lost at sea.

"I should have stayed in L.A. with Dad," Tiffany mumbled. "I could have moved into his apartment and not had to change schools."

Carly ignored that mostly because she didn't know what to say. In truth, Neil hadn't been interested in sharing custody of his daughter. It was as if once he'd decided to leave, his only child no longer existed for him. Carly couldn't understand that, but in the past few weeks she'd realized that Neil had become a stranger to her. Maybe he always had been. Maybe she'd been fooling herself throughout their marriage.

What she didn't know was how it was possible to live with a man for sixteen years, have his child, sleep with him, talk to him, plan a future with him and find out she'd been wrong about almost everything. Her mind spun every time she thought about it.

"Are we there yet?" Tiffany asked.

Carly chuckled. At last a question she could answer. "About another forty minutes."

Now that they were north of San Francisco, Carly found herself studying the changing landscape. The Northern California coastline was as rugged as it was beautiful. She remembered the narrow, rocky beaches, the high cliffs, the storms that would blow through. But mostly, she remembered the beautiful bed-and-breakfast/house where she'd grown up.

Chatsworth-by-the-Sea had once been an elegant English manor with a different name. Her great-great—however many greats—grandfather had made his fortune during the gold rush in the 1850s. Determined to leave a legacy, he'd bought a massive house in England and had it brought over stone by stone.

For Carly, Chatsworth-by-the-Sea had always been *home*. With everything going on in her life, she longed to return to the comfortable welcome she'd always found there. And yet she felt unsettled.

"I can't wait to see the old place again," she said. "You always liked it, too."

Tiffany shrugged. "To visit. I never thought we'd live there. Is Grandma going to make us do work and stuff?"

"You'll have a few chores, but nothing worse than you had before." Carly almost said "at home" but stopped herself in time. The last thing she needed was Tiffany in tears again. Her daughter's blue eyes were still swollen from that morning's crying jag.

Not that Tiffany was the only one upset about leaving behind their house in Santa Monica. Change was never easy. Given the choice, Carly would have stayed put. But she hadn't had a choice. The difference was she'd kept her pain and sadness to herself. After all, she was the mom and it was up to her to be the strong one. Carly didn't mind that so much. What made things really hard was the sense of being trapped by circumstances she couldn't control.

"Are you going to run the bed-and-breakfast for Grandma?" Tiffany asked.

"That's the plan. I'll learn the family business and take over responsibilities. In two years, Grandma will move to Las Vegas."

Carly's mother had already bought a town house in a complex she liked and was renting it out until she was ready to retire there. After Rhonda left for the wilds of Nevada, Carly would claim the wonderful B and B as her own. She would have a secure job, an income and an inheritance to leave her daughter. It was really the perfect solution for everyone.

Carly knew she should be grateful that everything had worked out so well. She had a job and a place for her and her daughter to live, while her mother would be able to move somewhere warm and go to bingo every day.

So why did she feel so lousy? Why did it seem that less than two months from turning forty, her life was already over?

"What would Grandma have done if you and Dad hadn't split up?" Tiffany asked. "Would we still have moved here to run things?"

"I don't know what would have happened," Carly said, which was both true and a lie. She and Neil had never discussed the fate of the B and B because he'd made it more than clear he wasn't interested. But there was no way Carly would have let her mother sell it. Not after it had been in the family nearly a hundred and fifty years.

"I still would rather live in Santa Monica," Tiffany said. "It was great there. This is going to be totally gross."

"'Gross' is harsh. I know moving to a small town is going to be different for you," Carly told her daughter. "But there's still a lot to do. The mall's not that far away. There are movie theaters and lots of after-school activities."

Tiffany wrinkled her nose, but didn't speak.

"I had a favorite place high in one of the towers," Carly continued. "I used to take a book up there and read on rainy afternoons."

"Oh, yeah, *that* sounds thrilling."

So much sarcasm dripped off the words that Carly half expected to see a puddle on the car mat.

"There's also the ghost," she reminded her daughter.

Tiffany only looked bored. "I never saw the ghost except for that stupid painting in the dining room. Are you sure it's real? I don't think anyone believes in ghosts anymore, Mom."

"I do. At least I did when I was your age." The ghost was one of Carly's favorite memories from growing up. Like the way the house looked at Christmas or on a stormy night.

In truth, she was willing to admit that while the ghost had been very real to her when she'd been Tiffany's age, now she had a little more trouble believing. But she wasn't willing to let the idea go completely.

"I used to read up in the tower room and sometimes I'd look up and see a pale, shimmering essence right there, next to me."

"I don't think a 'shimmering essence' counts as an actual ghost, Mom," Tiffany said. "Besides, Daddy always said it was bogus. Whoever heard of a ghost named Mary?"

"He never came to the B and B, so he wouldn't know. We're in all the ghost registries, including the national one. They're very fussy about who they register. Chatsworth-by-the-Sea is famous for our spectral phenomena. We've had scientists and ghostbusters visiting for as long as the house has been here. No one has ever been able to prove there *wasn't* a ghost."

Tiffany frowned. "But she's like nice, right?"

"Of course."

"I don't want her hanging around when I'm getting dressed and stuff."

Carly grinned. "I thought you didn't believe in ghosts."

"I don't. But maybe, I don't know, there's something." Tiffany glanced at Carly. "How did she die?"

"I don't know. We couldn't find out that information about her. I know your great-grandmother did a lot of research on Mary and never discovered much about her. The theory is she somehow came over with the house. The documentation about her says her clothes appear to be from the Regency era. That's around 1811. She's young—maybe twenty-two or so. She likes flowers."

"How do you know?"

"I saw her in the garden once." Or she'd seen something. It had been close to midnight, on a perfect summer evening. Carly had been around her daughter's age and hating life as much as Tiffany did when things didn't go her way. She'd been crying and there'd been some kind of…

"More shimmering essence?" Tiffany asked.

"Yeah." It could have been moonlight or shadows.

Tiffany shook her head. "She's not *real*."

"I know, but she's still entitled to her privacy."

Carly shrugged. Okay. Maybe it *was* a stretch to think there was a real ghost, but the possibility was there. To her mind Mary had always been a wary and benevolent presence. Almost a friend. After all she'd been through, Carly figured she needed all the friends she could get.

As soon as she and Neil had started telling people they were getting a divorce, Carly had been stunned by all the supposed friends who had disappeared from her life. It was as if she had a contagious disease they were desperate to avoid. Suddenly women she'd known for years weren't returning her calls and were too busy to have lunch. She'd felt more and more isolated. Then Neil had moved out and Tiffany had gotten even more difficult.

When Carly's mother had called to offer her the chance to take over the B and B, Carly had accepted. Moving north would give Tiffany a chance to finish her education in an excellent high school in a charming town. Carly could still work full-time while being around for her daughter. Both of them would have a chance to start over.

The only potentially troubling aspect of the plan was that

Carly and her mother had never exactly been close. There was too much friction between them.

"I'll make it work," Carly murmured. She had to. There weren't a lot of other options.

"Are you talking to yourself?" her daughter asked.

"Yes. Does it make you nervous?"

"No. It's just weird."

"Which you expect from me," Carly said.

"Pretty much."

Carly nodded. Not a surprise. She'd always wanted to be one of those cool moms, but somehow she hadn't figured out how. If being cool meant letting her daughter get her belly button pierced or stay out until midnight or date older guys, then Carly was willing to be weird and difficult.

They exited the highway and turned toward the ocean. Chatsworth-by-the-Sea stood on the edge of a cliff overlooking the Pacific. Wooden steps led down to the beach below. There were beautiful grounds, a few hardy vineyards and some fruit trees, but for Carly, nothing compared with the wonder of being able to watch the ever-changing ocean. She liked storms best, although sunny days were great, too.

"This is going to be a lot of fun," she said to Tiffany. "You'll see."

"Fun for you, maybe. You're getting everything you want. I'm getting nothing and it's your fault I don't have my dad anymore. I hate you."

The unfairness of the accusation burned Carly down to her bones. As Tiffany began to cry softly into a tissue, Carly had to fight her own pain. Oh, yeah, this was everything she'd ever wanted. Running a bed-and-breakfast, living with her mother and daughter, trapped in a life that wasn't the one she'd chosen. She was making the best of a bad situation. She was doing most of this *for* Tiffany so her daughter could have a sense of place and belonging.

Carly considered several responses, and tossed them all away. Sometimes the better course of action was to suck it up and wait it out, which is what she decided to do. But once, just once, she would like someone to consider *her* feelings. She would like someone to take responsibility, to do the right thing and let her have the tantrum.

She drove down the familiar street and reminded herself that she would soon be back in the house where she grew up. At least she would have her mother to help. The burdens wouldn't be hers alone.

"We're nearly there," she told her daughter. "If you're crying, Grandma's going to have about fifty thousand questions."

"I know." Tiffany sniffed, then wiped her face. "I just wish you'd been a better wife."

As far as knife wounds went, this one cut right to Carly's heart. But before she could catch her breath, or think of a response, they'd pulled into the large gravel parking lot to the side of the massive four-story building that was Chatsworth-by-the-Sea.

Carly parked next to her mother's Jeep and turned off the engine. The pain faded as she studied the stone structure, the climbing ivy, the old and familiar trees. She could see the first of the towers.

"We're here," she said, as if Tiffany wouldn't notice the big house in front of them. "Let's go find Grandma."

Right now what Carly needed more than anything was a hug and a promise that everything would be all right. She wanted to drink cocoa and eat cookies and pretend she was Tiffany's age and the biggest problem she had was fitting in at school.

"Just leave the luggage for now," Carly said as she climbed out of the car. "We can get it later."

The crunch of her feet on the gravel made her smile. The sound was familiar, as was the scent of flowers and sea and something undefinable but old that had always made her think of home. Because it *was* home. It was simpler, easier times—when the world still made sense.

She led the way through the side yard where herbs and vegetables grew to a wooden door that led through the mudroom into the kitchen. At this time of day, her mother would be preparing the appetizers that were served from four-thirty to six.

"Hi, Mom, it's us," Carly called as she walked into the large, airy kitchen.

Rhonda Washington stood at the wide center island, cutting slices of cheese. She glanced up when her daughter and granddaughter entered, smiled and put down her knife.

"How was the drive? You made excellent time. Tiffany, you're growing up to be so beautiful. Did your mom feed you something decent or have you been living on junk food all day?"

"Hi, Grandma."

Tiffany stepped into the offered hug and didn't answer the question. Carly ignored the flash of irritation and told herself that her mother hadn't meant it as a criticism. Not really.

To distract herself, she studied the different generations of women, noting that Tiffany was a couple of inches taller, but that they shared both bone structure and eye color.

Rhonda had been born blond. Over time the color had darkened to a light brown, only to fade into gray. Tiffany's pale blond had yet to darken at all, although Carly suspected it would with time. But the similarities didn't end there. Both of them had the same smile and ability to speak their minds in a way that left her dodging bullets.

A small price to pay for sanctuary, Carly reminded herself.

Rhonda kissed her granddaughter on the cheek, then turned to Carly. "How's my baby girl?"

"Good, Mom. I'm doing okay."

"Are you sure?"

Eyes as blue as her own studied her face. Carly offered a smile she was pretty sure looked sincere and even normal, then stepped into her mother's embrace. Familiar scents and memories enveloped her. Her mother's insistence on wearing Chanel No. 5 perfume every single day of her life. The warmth in the hug.

"It's good to have you here," Rhonda said.

"It's good to *be* here."

They straightened. Carly noted there were a few more lines around her mother's eyes and mouth, a slight drooping at her shoulders, but otherwise she looked much as she always had. The Washington women seemed to have sturdy genes, a fact Carly appreciated as she stood less than two months from turning forty.

"Let's get you two settled," Rhonda said. "I'm so excited that we're going to be living together. Three generations in the same house. It will be like the Waltons."

"The who?" Tiffany asked as she snagged a slice of cheese.

"Some old show on TV," Carly told her. "A big family living in one house. They all said good-night to John-Boy. You sort of had to be there."

Tiffany didn't look convinced by the thrill of the experience. "So where do we sleep? I have my own room, right? I mean I have to. I'm fifteen, Grandma."

"I know. It's amazing how fast you're growing. Of course you have your own room. Two rooms, really. I picked them out especially for you. I think you'll really like them. They're in the tower."

Tiffany stiffened. "The one with the ghost?"

Her grandmother drew her eyebrows together. "No, dear. Not by the ghost. What a silly question. Carly, honey, you're on the third floor in one of the older rooms. You can pick something else if you'd like."

"I'm sure it will be fine," Carly said, knowing that "older room" wasn't a euphemism. No doubt the room her mother had picked for her hadn't been refurbished in close to a hundred years.

While the working section of the B and B had twenty-five bedrooms and five suites, the house had closer to forty. Some were too small to be used for guests. Others were in noisy areas, or didn't get any light. When the house had been converted from a private residence to a B and B in the 1930s, some bedrooms had been held back for family.

Carly followed her mother to the old-fashioned elevator that took them to the third floor. From there they had to walk to the tower staircase.

"Are you going to be comfortable here on your own?" Carly asked her daughter.

Tiffany's response was to roll her eyes and sigh heavily.

"She's not a child," Rhonda said crisply. "She's an independent young woman who needs her privacy."

"See," Tiffany said as she raised her chin. "Grandma doesn't think I'm a child."

Carly knew there was no point having *that* conversation. She went up the stairs to the narrow door that led to the tower rooms.

"Isn't this terrific?" Rhonda asked as she opened the door and stepped inside.

Originally three rooms had made up the tower. The

smallest had been converted into a bathroom. The other two consisted of a small bedroom and a sitting room.

"I brought up a desk so you have a place to study," Rhonda said. "The bedspread is new and the wallpaper is only a few years old. Of course we can replace it all if you'd like."

Tiffany walked through the rooms. "They're great," she said, sounding delighted and surprised.

Carly agreed with both assessments. This tower faced south, so it got a lot of light. There were windows in both rooms, with the one in the sitting area looking out over the ocean.

The bright floral-print wallpaper provided a cheerful color palate played out in the rooms. The bedspread was lavender, the desk-chair cushion pink and the club chair and ottoman had been done in periwinkle. Thick carpeting covered what had been hardwood floors.

Instead of a closet, each room had an armoire. The bathroom was tiny but functional. There were bookcases, shelves and what signified true joy in any teenager's life—a phone.

"I love it!" her daughter said happily as she moved from one room to the other. "I love everything about it."

Carly winced. She was happy that Tiffany was pleased, but a little wounded that she couldn't be the one to provide the joy.

Rhonda pointed to the phone. "Your own line. I wrote the phone number down somewhere." She checked the pad on the desk and pointed to the top sheet. "Here it is. I got you a plan that gives you fifty dollars' worth of long distance a month so you can stay in touch with your old friends."

Tiffany's eyes filled with tears, but for once they were happy ones. "Oh, Grandma, you're the best." She hugged Rhonda.

Carly sighed with relief. She'd been afraid her daughter would hate everything about the house and the move, but finding such great digs at the end of the trip would go a long way to setting things right.

We may just survive this after all, she thought happily. Wouldn't that be great?

"Want to see your room?" her mother asked.

"Sure."

They went back the way they'd come, taking the stairs down a floor. A large set of double doors closed off the guest section of the floor from the private part of the house. Rhonda went through one of them and walked to the end of the corridor.

Here the house was much older and not nearly so shiny. There was dust in the corners and bits of backing showing through the carpet.

"I picked a corner room to give you more light," her mother said as she opened the last door on the right.

Carly stepped into a big room with windows on two walls. The furniture was old—original Art Deco style—which she loved. The bedspread looked new and out of place with the gleaming wood, but she figured she could change that later. There was a big armoire, a desk in the corner and a chair pulled up in front of the window facing the ocean.

"It's great," she said.

"Are you sure?" Her mother sounded worried. "I know it's not new. Usually when you visit you stay in one of the guest rooms and they're much nicer."

"It's fine," Carly assured her. "I'll enjoy the quiet." She knew her mother kept a suite of rooms on the first floor.

"Good."

Tiffany glanced around. "Where's the bathroom?"

"Down the hall," Rhonda said. "But she doesn't have to share it."

"Cool. I'll go get my stuff and start taking it upstairs," Tiffany said as she bolted for the door. "When will the truck arrive?"

Most of their furniture had been sold, but they'd kept a few things.

"Tomorrow," Carly told her. "Think you can survive without your TV until then?"

"Oh, Mom. Of course I can. I'm not totally worthless."

Tiffany ran down the hallway toward the elevator. Carly walked to the window and stared out.

"It's the same view," she said, feeling the pain and uncertainty fade away. Coming back to the B and B had made sense. Of the very few choices open to her, this one had the most opportunity for success. If it wasn't the life she would have chosen, so what? At least she had a place to go and someone to help her get back on her feet.

"I'm glad you're here," her mother said.

"Me, too. The past couple of months have been a nightmare, but it's all behind us now. Tiffany and I can start over. I really appreciate the opportunity, Mom."

"Yes, well, this has always been your home. I'm just glad you wanted to come here so I didn't have to sell the place."

Carly turned to her mother. "You wouldn't really have done that, would you?"

"Oh, it's so big and a lot of work. I'm not getting any younger."

"But you have your staff. It's not as if you're cleaning rooms yourself."

"I know, but there are responsibilities." Her mother cleared her throat. "People aren't traveling the way they used to. In my day, travel was an adventure. Now most folks would rather sit home and watch cable." She shrugged. "But that's all right. Now that you're here, we'll get things on track."

Carly didn't like the sound of that. "What do you mean?"

"There have been a few lean years. I've wanted to make some repairs—needed to, really—but I couldn't. This is your legacy, Carly. It makes sense to invest in it."

The cold, dark panic of the past two months returned. Invest? What did she mean *invest?* "What are you talking about, Mom? Is the B and B in financial trouble?"

Rhonda avoided eye contact, instead giving the bedspread an unnecessary tug. "Just a little. But with your divorce settlement, we can get on our feet financially."

If Carly had been able to breathe, she would have laughed. As it was she could only stare in disbelief. She'd come here seeking safety and security, but apparently that was not to be.

"You had all the equity in the house," Rhonda continued. "Neil had that great job for all those years. I know you probably don't want to tap into your savings, but you'll earn it back. Plus you have the alimony and child support. We'll be fine."

Carly's chest tightened. "Mom, there's no money. No savings, no house equity. I got half of everything, including half of the debts. I couldn't afford to stay in L.A. That's why I came here."

CHAPTER 2

"You're wrong," her mother said. "There has to be money. You're just being ridiculous, and selfish." Disapproval tightened her face. "I expected you to be more mature about everything."

Carly opened her mouth, then closed it. She'd been home all of four minutes. Maybe she and her mother could put off fighting for at least an hour.

"Let's talk about this later," Carly said with a smile. "Right now I'm just happy to see you."

Rhonda didn't look mollified but she didn't speak, either. Probably because they could hear Tiffany heading toward them. The teenager clumped down the two back stairs and entered the bedroom.

"Mom, I brought one of your suitcases."

"Thanks."

Tiffany shrugged. "It was on top of mine. Anyway, there's tons more stuff."

They spent the next fifteen minutes unloading the car. Carly went up to Tiffany's room to make sure she had started unpacking, only to be told by her daughter that she wasn't a baby and could manage emptying a suitcase without supervision.

"Feel the love," Carly murmured as she walked down one floor to her room and stepped inside.

The view captured her attention instantly. She crossed to the window and stared out at the ocean. Living in Santa Monica had meant they were within a couple miles of the water, but nothing compared with living so close to the vastness. She loved how the colors changed with the variations in light and weather. The water could be dark blue one minute, then gray, then nearly black, then almost turquoise. As a teenager, when it had seemed her world would never be right, she could always count on the ocean.

After unpacking her clothes and putting them in the dresser and hanging a few things in the armoire, she walked downstairs and into the main rooms of the B and B. There was a parlor to the left of the big, open foyer. Sofas and chairs sat in groups in a semicircle around the big fireplace. She noted the furnishings were exactly as she remembered, although the hardwood floors looked as if they'd been refinished not that long ago.

On the other side of the foyer was the dining room. A long table that seated fourteen stood in the center of the space. Several smaller tables seating four or six were up against the walls. There were large windows that overlooked the grounds and the ocean beyond. A portrait of Mary hung opposite the window.

Carly ran her hand along the main table, liking the smooth feel of the wood and how the carvings reminded her of days spent doing her homework in this room. Three large chandeliers provided overhead light in the evening—the cut glass casting shadows that had made her think of foreign lands and battles with dragons and being a princess.

So many memories, she thought. Most of them happy. Had that changed?

She walked to the office area and checked on the board. Only four of the twenty-five rooms were occupied. Carly frowned. Sure, it was midweek, but it was spring break. Shouldn't the B and B be more busy?

She headed for the kitchen where her mother had put out two bottles of wine. With so few guests, they wouldn't need more than a couple.

Maybe she could sneak one upstairs into her room and

drown her sorrows, she thought glumly. A nice cabernet sauvignon and some chocolate could go a long way to making her feel more perky about her life.

"All settled?" her mother asked.

"I'm unpacked," Carly said, not sure how long it would take to feel settled. Between Neil walking out, having to sell the house, moving and starting over with a life she wasn't sure she wanted, she didn't think "settled" was on the agenda.

"Something smells good," Carly said as she moved to the oven and pulled it open.

"Maribel made those this morning," her mother said. "They should be about done. Do the crusts look brown?"

As Carly checked out the mini quiches, her mouth began to water. "They look perfect." She reached for the hot pad on the counter and pulled the two trays out of the oven.

"I'm glad Maribel is still working here," she said, pleased to know there would be at least one friendly face in residence.

"I'd be lost without her," Rhonda said. "She knows it, too. She's always after me for a raise, and as badly as things are going here, I don't see how she has the nerve."

Carly took a step back. Okay, not a conversation she wanted to have her first day here. At least not the part about Maribel. But she was going to have to get the rest of it straightened out at some point, and why not now?

"When did things start going badly, Mom?" she asked as she slipped the mini quiches onto a cooling rack. "You never mentioned anything to me."

"I didn't want to worry you. I knew you had your hands full with Neil. Besides, what could you do from all the way down there?"

Technically there was nothing wrong with what her mother had said, Carly told herself. If she put those three sentences in front of an impartial jury, they would tell her that her mother was being sensitive and stating the obvious. Most likely Rhonda *hadn't* wanted to worry her daughter, and Carly had had her hands full with Neil. As for being far away, it was true, too.

However, this wasn't an impartial jury, and in the momspeak Carly knew so well, what Rhonda had just said was: "You're too busy for me, as always. Sure I could have told you what was going on, but you were always more interested in your husband, who left you, by the way. Of course being so far away meant I was totally on my own. But you're selfish and I'm used to that."

"You can tell me now," Carly said, proud of how calm she sounded. "What's up with the B and B? I would have thought it would be more full, what with it being spring break."

Her mother glared at her. "Oh, sure. Be critical of how I run things. What happened with you? What do you mean there isn't any money from the divorce? There has to be. Neil made a lot of money in his marketing job."

So they were going to talk about her failure, Carly thought. Might as well get it over with.

"Neil did well," she admitted. "My job didn't pay so much." The office manager position with a single-doctor practice didn't pull in the big bucks. "We were careful to put money aside for Tiffany's college, but after that, Neil lost interest. We took all those expensive vacations, then there were the cars."

Neil had liked to lease a new one every two years. The monthly payment for their last Mercedes had cost more than their food bill. She'd hated that and had protested, but Neil had pointed out that it was important for him to have a car that matched his position in the company. Carly had tried to argue the point with him, but he'd told her she couldn't possibly understand. That had felt so much like being patted on the head, that she'd yelled at him. Then they'd had a big fight. In the end, he'd gotten the car anyway.

"We put in the new landscaping last year," she said. "There were other things we bought. In hindsight I should have pushed back more on the budget. The bottom line is, by the time we split everything, I owned half of nothing."

"But the house," her mother protested. "That had to be worth a fortune."

"It was. And we owed nearly as much."

Carly didn't know how to explain that it had been easier to give in to Neil than to fight him all the time.

"You were raised better than that," her mother said.

"Not helpful," Carly told her.

"Don't you get alimony?"

"Yes, and no. Neil quit his job. Until he gets a new one, he doesn't have to pay. He owes child support, although that's on a sliding scale. Basically if he gets back into marketing at the level he was at, he's going to be passing about half his salary on to me for alimony and child support. That doesn't give him much incentive to start looking."

"I think this is all just wrong," her mother said as she set the serving trays on the counter. "In my day a man knew his responsibilities. Your father never left me. He wasn't that kind of man. You should have thought about that when you married Neil. I never liked him, you know."

"Mmm." Carly went for the noncommittal response.

What was she going to say? That both her parents had adored Neil from the second she'd brought him home? That for the first two years of their marriage she'd joked that if she and Neil split up, her parents would want custody of *him?*

"You used to have a good job," her mother said. "What happened to that?"

"The events planning? That was a million years ago." She tested one of the quiches to see if it had cooled enough, then began sliding them onto a serving plate.

"You should never have given up your career," her mother said. "If you'd kept up with it, you wouldn't be in trouble now."

"Agreed, but it was too difficult to handle big parties and corporate events once I had Tiffany. I wanted to be home more."

"At least you got that right," her mother told her. "You needed to be there."

Carly felt as if she were in a fun house. Could her mother just pick a side and stay on it? Any side. At this point Carly didn't even care if it was one in which she was the villain.

She handed over the plate of quiche.

"I don't know what we're going to do," Rhonda said as she set the plate on the tray. "I thought you'd be able to put some money into the B and B. But if you can't..."

She stopped talking and pressed her lips together. Carly watched her. They were family, she thought sadly. Shouldn't they be able to pull together on this?

Obviously her fantasy of coming home and finding everything in her world put to rights wasn't going to happen.

"I suppose I could sell," her mother said as she walked to the cupboard and pulled down several wineglasses. "I still have a lot of equity in this place. We could use it to buy you something in Las Vegas. Or I could sell my town house and we could buy a larger place together."

Carly figured she would rather be tied naked to a fire-ant hill. She'd known moving back to the B and B would mean sharing relatively close quarters with her mother, but there had been a time limit. In two years, Rhonda would head off to her retirement. Carly would run the B and B and send her mother a monthly check for her share of the business. It wasn't a perfect solution or one she would have chosen, but it solved so many problems.

However, living with her mother on a permanent basis was something else entirely.

"This house has been in the family for nearly a hundred and fifty years," Carly said. "You can't be serious about selling it."

"I'm not sure there's a choice."

"There has to be another way," she said, not sure what it could be, but determined to find it. "This is a lot of information. I need to think about it all."

"Be my guest," her mother said. "I've been worrying for seven years."

Carly refused to translate *that* into momspeak.

"Of course you and Neil may work everything out and get back together," Rhonda added.

"Unlikely," Carly said. "Not only wouldn't I take him back, but I can't imagine anything making him want to go back to his old life."

"I'm so sorry, dear."

Her mother patted her arm.

Carly frowned. "Sorry about what?"

"That Neil left you for someone else. Is she much younger and prettier?"

Carly didn't know if she should laugh or cry. "No, Mom. Neil didn't leave me for anyone. There's no other woman. He just wanted to go find himself."

Carly escaped to her room after dinner. Tiffany was going to watch TV with her grandmother and Carly took the opportunity to sneak away.

It wasn't that she didn't want to be with her family, it was that she needed time to think. Nothing had turned out the way she'd thought and that was going to take some getting used to.

At night the ocean was a blanket of darkness. She opened the windows, and although she couldn't see waves or even whitecaps, the sound of the sea was audible and she could smell the salt air. At least *that* was as she remembered. But the rest of it—not so much.

Carly settled on the window seat and stared into the darkness. At what point had her life taken this unexpected turn? Had there been signs along the way? Had she simply not been paying attention? Sure, things with Neil hadn't been great for a while, but it hadn't occurred to her that divorce was an option. They had a child together; there had been vows. She'd chosen to spend her life with him and a few disappointments along the way hadn't been a reason to change her mind.

So why had he changed his? Had his experience been worse than hers, or had he not believed in the "forever" part of their marriage? Was she a fool for staying so long, or was he a jerk for leaving? Did the truth lie somewhere in the middle?

She wasn't sure it mattered. After all, they were divorcing now and both starting over. Neil had his dreams and she had… Carly sighed. She had no clue what she had. A teenage daughter who would rather live with her father, a mother who had kept the news of the failing business from her only child, and a future that looked far too uncertain.

Which meant Carly didn't have a lot of options. Either she stayed and fought for the B and B or she left and started over somewhere else. While she'd been working steadily for the past twenty years, she wasn't sure her recent job qualified her for much. Sure she'd run an office, but it had been small and the paycheck had matched.

Eighteen years ago things had been different. She'd been a successful events planner and she'd loved the work. In three years she'd risen to the top, with a list of clients that made her competition weep. But then she'd had Tiffany, and the sixty- to seventy-hour workweeks and constant late nights had been impossible with a baby.

In an effort to balance her love of event planning with having a husband and a baby, she'd turned to wedding planning. While the hours had been better, Neil had hated her being gone nearly every weekend. In truth, she'd never seen him. So she'd quit that, too, and had found the office manager job.

Could she go back to events planning? Unfortunately she hadn't kept in touch with many of her old friends from the business. Plus she wouldn't like the hours anymore now than she had when Tiffany had been a baby. One of the reasons she'd come to the B and B was so that she could be around for her daughter. These last three years before she went off to college were important and Carly didn't want to miss them.

But she also had a responsibility to put food on the table and a roof over their heads. If events planning wasn't an option and L.A. was too expensive and she wasn't staying here, then she would need to look at moving somewhere else. There had to be places with a less crazy cost of living.

If only she had—

A soft knock on her door brought her to her feet. Carly crossed the floor and pulled open the door. Tiffany stood in front of her. The teen wore teddy bear pajamas and carried a tattered stuffed dog in her arms.

"What's up?" Carly asked.

"Nothing." Tiffany shrugged as she stepped inside. "My room is great. It's just..." She shrugged. "You know."

"It's a little creepy up there?"

Tiffany dropped her chin. "Maybe a little. I'll be completely fine," she added quickly. "I love my room. I just thought, you know, for the first night."

Carly glanced at the large bed, then closed the door. "Sure, you can sleep with me."

"Good."

Tiffany ran and jumped on the bed. "I took the back stairs. It's really weird because the house is so quiet, but there are all these noises."

"Old places are known for that."

"It made me think of the ghost. Not that she's real."

Carly stretched out in the bed. Tiffany set her dog on the nightstand, then shimmied under the blankets. She snuggled close and rested her head on Carly's shoulder.

"Grandma was pretty cool tonight," the teenager said. "We watched HBO together."

"Nothing R-rated, right?"

"Oh, Mo-om. You're so old."

"Grandma's older than me."

"Yeah, but she's more fun."

Carly tried not to take the comment personally. As her daughter's mother, it was her job to be a parent, not a buddy. But just once she would like someone else to be the bad guy for a while. Neil was never willing to take on that task. Of course, he'd never bothered all that much with his daughter, despite the fact that Tiffany adored him.

She stretched up and turned off the light, then settled back on the bed. Tiffany sighed.

"Where do you think Daddy is?" she asked, almost as if she knew her mother had been thinking of Neil.

"I don't know. I thought he was going to stay in L.A. for a while. Until he bought his boat."

"Do you think he's really going to sail to Hawaii?"

"That's what he said."

"Wow. It's so far. And there aren't any, like, places to stop."

"I'm sure he'll take a good map."

Carly did her best to keep the bitterness out of her voice. Neil got to buy a boat and run off to Hawaii while she was left behind to be the grown-up. Again.

"Do you think…" Tiffany hesitated, then swallowed. "Do you think he misses me?"

"Of course he does. You're his best girl."

"I guess. It's just he never wanted to, you know, spend time with me, and he hasn't called since he left."

"He'll call," Carly said, then vowed she would find Neil and force him to call his daughter. Damn the man for being such an insensitive bastard, she thought grimly. How could he do this to Tiffany? She could try to forgive a lot of things, but never that.

She wrapped her arms around Tiffany and squeezed. "He's going through a lot right now. But he'll settle into his new life and you can be a part of it. That will be fun."

"Yeah. We can go sailing together."

"Good idea."

Tiffany sighed. "It's nice here. I kinda didn't want to come because I thought it would be way stupid, but I like the house. You're not going to make me clean rooms, are you?"

"We'll negotiate a chore list," Carly said. "The maids make pretty good money."

"How good?"

"Let's talk in the morning."

"Okay. Night."

"Night, baby. I love you."

"I love you, too, Mom."

Carly listened to her daughter's breathing. It didn't take very long for it to slow and get very deep. When Tiffany was asleep, Carly tried to memorize everything about this moment—how her daughter clung to her even in sleep, the way her hair smelled, the feel of her thin arms. There wouldn't be many more nights when Tiffany needed to sleep with her mom to feel safe, and Carly didn't want to miss a moment of what might be the last one.

"They grow up too fast," she whispered.

CHAPTER 3

Carly woke up to a morning so beautiful, she couldn't help but feel optimistic about the day and her future. She left her daughter asleep and went downstairs to fire up her morning with a jumbo mug of coffee. Sunshine, the smell of the ocean and a jolt of caffeine. Did it get any better than that?

She took the back stairs instead of the elevator and enjoyed the play of light on the old paneling. Even the servants had had a view, she thought humorously as she walked across the landing and glanced out at the expanse of gardens below. When she reached the main floor, she headed for the kitchen. If she hadn't been sure of her destination, the mouthwatering scent of cinnamon and something baking would have drawn her in.

Anticipation quickened her steps. Not just for the

yummy stuff, but also to see Maribel. Although they talked regularly by phone, she hadn't seen her friend in over a year.

"Hey, you," Carly said as she opened the kitchen door and stepped inside. "You're up early."

Maribel pulled something out of the oven, straightened, turned and grinned. "You made it!"

Carly waited until her friend put down the baking sheet, then approached. She opened her arms wide for a hug, only to come to a complete stop and stare.

"You're…you're…"

Maribel laughed, then smoothed the front of her white chef's coat over her belly. "Pregnant. I know."

"But… You can't be. You're…"

Carly didn't know what to say. "Too old," came to mind. As she and Maribel were practically the same age, her friend was also within weeks of turning forty.

"You didn't say anything," Carly told her instead.

"I know." Maribel moved close and hugged her. "When I found out about the baby, you and Neil had already started talking about the divorce. I didn't know if I should share my news or not. Then when you mentioned coming here, I figured I'd tell you in person. Don't be mad at me. I was seriously torn."

"I'm not mad. I couldn't be. I'll admit to being stunned. A baby. Wow."

Carly squeezed her, then stepped back. She studied her friend's bright, happy expression and the blush on her cheeks. Always petite and curvy, Maribel now defined lush. Her new shorter haircut emphasized her pretty features.

"You look amazing. Seriously, you're doing the glowing thing. But a baby? Are you excited?"

"I am now," Maribel admitted. "But at first it was a real shock. Only Dani's still in high school, the other three are in college. Pete and I figured we were finally going to buy that RV and see the world. Or at least the part we can drive to. Then this happened."

She touched her stomach. "I cried for three days when the doctor told me I didn't have the flu. Then I had a dream I wasn't pregnant and I woke myself up crying because I was so sad. That's when I figured I really *did* want the baby."

Carly nodded, even though she didn't understand. She and Maribel had gone different ways—Carly had attended college for a couple of years before starting in events planning and Maribel had married right out of high school. She'd had her first child on her twentieth birthday.

"Tiffany's fifteen," she said. "I can't imagine starting over with a newborn now."

"The kids are still getting over the shock," Maribel said as she walked to the island and began cutting up strawberries. "I suspect it's a whole lot more about Mom and Dad having sex than the actual idea of a baby."

"Pregnant," Carly said, still trying to take it in. Talk about a life change. "You're putting my divorce in perspective. When are you due?"

"Four more months."

Carly eyed her friend's large stomach. "Really?"

Maribel laughed. "Yeah, I know. I'm huge. I've always carried big, but this time I swear it's part elephant."

Carly walked over to the baking pan and stared at the cinnamon rolls. "Want me to take these out?"

"That would be great. So, enough about me and my surprise. How are you doing?"

"Okay. It's weird to be back."

Maribel dumped the cut strawberries into the fruit bowl. "Have you talked to your mom about anything?" she asked, sounding neutral.

Carly appreciated the sensitivity. "If you're asking if she's already mentioned that she wants me to use my divorce settlement to rescue the B and B, then yes. If it's something else, I'm not sure I could handle it."

"No, it's the money thing," Maribel said. "She's been really anxious for you to arrive. It's all she talks about."

Carly didn't consider that especially good news. "It's the week before Easter," she said. "Shouldn't we be busier?"

"Things have been slow for a while," Maribel admitted. "Bookings are dropping off. My food order is about half what it was this time last year."

"As bad as that," Carly said quietly. So much for hoping her mother had been exaggerating the situation.

A timer *dinged*. Maribel moved to the second oven and pulled out a pan of muffins. Carly drew in a deep breath.

"Those smell heavenly, too. Now I don't know which I want."

"Have one of each," Maribel urged.

"I'd love to, but I don't have the cash flow to replace my wardrobe with a larger size." One of the joys of getting older, Carly thought. She could no longer eat whatever she wanted and still fit into her clothes. Soon she was going to have to get serious about organized exercise, and how twisted was that?

"Do you have any big plans for the B and B?" Maribel asked. "Your mom thought you might."

Carly sensed her friend's interest was more than casual. No doubt she wanted to keep her job. The hours were perfect for someone with children and Maribel had always loved cooking.

"Not off the top of my head," Carly admitted. "I didn't think I would have to jump in to rescue a failing business my first day back."

Actually she'd planned on relaxing a little, basking in the whole "moving back home" thing. But apparently not.

"It would be a shame to lose all this," Maribel said.

Carly agreed. Did she want to save it, and if she did, could she?

They both turned at the sound of footsteps in the hallway. Tiffany pushed open the swinging door and smiled shyly.

"Hi," she said. "You got up way early."

Carly glanced at the clock and raised her eyebrows. "So did you. You remember my friend Maribel, don't you?"

"Uh-huh. Hi." Tiffany inhaled. "I remember your muffins, too. You're the best cook."

"Aren't you sweet for saying so." Maribel grabbed a paper towel and pulled one of the muffins out of the pan. "Be careful," she said as she handed it to Tiffany. "They're still hot."

"Thanks. I'm going to walk around outside," Tiffany said.

"Have fun," Carly told her. She wanted to add something about not going too far, or staying away from the main road, but she held back. Her daughter was smart enough to know all that and right now Carly couldn't face another eye roll.

The back door slammed shut behind her. Maribel sighed. "She's beautiful and she looks a whole lot more grown-up than fifteen."

"Tell me about it. Older guys are constantly asking her out and I'm stuck trying to explain why this isn't a good thing."

"It gets worse," Maribel said cheerfully. "But then it gets better. Of course just when they settle down enough that you want to spend more time with them, they go off to college. Isn't that the way?"

"I don't remember being *that* much trouble," Carly grumbled.

"Me, either, but I'm guessing we were. Remember how we were going to change the world?" Maribel laughed. "I was going to live in Paris and become a world-class chef. You were going to marry a movie star and plan fabulous parties for all of Hollywood."

While Carly could remember talking endlessly about what she and Maribel had wanted to do with their lives, she had an odd feeling of being disconnected from the whole thing. As if it had been someone else dreaming those dreams.

Maribel picked up a kiwifruit and started peeling it.

"That was a long time ago. Funny how now I don't want anything but what I have."

Carly envied her friend her contentment. If pressed, Carly wasn't sure she could say what *she* wanted. Not anymore. Maybe not in a long time.

Carly put off unpacking to go online on her laptop. If she and Tiffany didn't stay here to make a go of things, they were going to need an alternate plan. But what? Her most recent occupation wasn't about to excite anyone and she didn't have the start-up capital or the savings to try going out on her own as an events planner.

She went to a couple of different cost-of-living Web sites and found out that she could indeed support herself and Tiffany on a doctor's office manager's salary in, say, Bakersfield. Or if they left the state. There were a lot of places cheaper to live in than Los Angeles.

If she wasn't at the B and B she wouldn't want to stay here. It would be too hard to be close to the house but not a part of it.

Is that what she wanted? To move somewhere new and start over without friends or family nearby? Not that there were all that many friends since the divorce. But still, there was the whole pain of leaving the familiar.

She left the Internet and went into the word-processing program. Maybe a list of pros and cons, she thought. Reasons to stay in L.A., reasons to stay and make the B and B work and reasons to locate elsewhere.

In Los Angeles, she had contacts, even if she hadn't used them in years. She might be able to land a job working for an events planner. Of course, as she reflected again, the hours *were* hideously long and she would be home while Tiffany was in school and gone the rest of the time.

If she stayed here, she would have to bring the B and B back from wherever it was and make it successful again. Which meant she needed to know how bad things were. As her mother wasn't the most forthcoming of information givers, Carly wasn't looking forward to *that* conversation. But staying meant being able to hang out with her daughter, to attend school functions, to be a mom.

Carly leaned back in her chair and closed her eyes. There were a thousand details to consider under any scenario. Like medical insurance. Getting it for Tiffany wouldn't be that difficult, but what about herself? Was she going to be considered "hard to insure" because of her age? And what about the fact that she would soon turn forty and have to check a different box on all those forms that asked for age in groups? Perhaps not relevant for her job search, but still depressing.

She looked back at her list. Obviously staying here was the best solution, assuming she could find a way to make it work.

Carly remembered growing up here. The B and B had always been crammed with guests. They were sold out for all the major holidays months in advance. There had been a wedding every Saturday from May through September. The holidays had been magical, with period decorations covering every inch of the public rooms. And she'd felt safe and happy, secure in the knowledge that she knew where she came from and where she was going.

"We could make that happen again," Carly told herself. "*I* could make it happen."

She had determination, drive and a willingness to do the hard work. Surely that would be enough. Which meant first up, she had to get accurate information from her mother.

Conveniently, Carly heard Rhonda calling for her. Unfortunately, Tiffany was also yelling for her, and the teenager didn't sound happy.

Carly saved the information and closed the computer program. Then she began the shut-down process as she yelled, "In here. What's going on?"

Tiffany marched in first. Her daughter looked upset and defiant. Tears sparkled in her eyes.

"Grandma's being mean," she announced.

"Your daughter is very spoiled and uncooperative," Rhonda said from behind the teenager.

Tiffany turned on the older woman. "You can't be serious. It's totally illegal to make me work so much. There are child labor laws. I know—I read about them in school. You can't exploit young workers for your own financial gain."

Rhonda's eyes widened with indignation. "I would think you'd be more grateful that I took you in, young lady. You're spoiled."

"Am not."

Carly stared at her daughter. "Tiffany, you're speaking to your grandmother."

Tiffany opened her mouth, then closed it. "She started it."

Rhonda looked smug. "You should have your daughter help more around the house. If she's part of the family, she needs to have responsibilities."

Carly wanted to reprimand her mother, too, but knew it wouldn't go over well.

"I blame you for this," Rhonda said.

Of course she did, Carly thought. When in doubt…

"Tiffany has always had chores," she said calmly. "We'll have to work some out for her." She frowned. Tiffany was fairly typical in having to be reminded to do her work, but she never absolutely refused. Plus, the girl had always liked her grandmother and wanted to hang out with her.

"What happened?" she asked.

Tiffany sniffed. "She told me to fold sheets."

Carly wanted to do an eye roll of her own. "The way you were talking, I expected to hear she put you to work sweeping the roof. It's just sheets. What's the problem?"

"It's *all* of them."

Carly didn't understand. "Not just the ones for your room?"

"Of course not. I'd do *that*." Her tone indicated that it wasn't possible for Carly to be more stupid. "I've never seen a pile this big. There were hundreds."

"Twenty or thirty sets," Rhonda said with a sniff. "You shouldn't exaggerate, Tiffany. It makes people think you're lying. I'm surprised your mother hasn't taught you that."

Carly ignored that. "Why so many sheets?"

"I haven't gotten around to folding them from the weekend," Rhonda said as she walked to the window and stared out at the view. "I've been busy."

Her mother's activities were the least of Carly's concerns. The real issue was why the housekeeping staff wasn't doing the laundry.

"Don't the housekeepers take care of the sheets on Tuesday?" she asked, knowing the staff was usually busy Monday, cleaning up from the weekend.

"They wash and dry them. I've been doing the folding."

Not good, Carly thought. She had more questions but didn't want to get into it in front of Tiffany.

She turned to her daughter. "We'll talk later today and come up with a chore list."

"You let her decide that sort of thing?" Rhonda asked, obviously annoyed.

"I think her input is important," Carly said. "But she doesn't decide."

"I could," Tiffany said defiantly. "I'd do a great job."

Carly narrowed her gaze. "This would be a great time for you to keep quiet."

Tiffany opened her mouth, then closed it. "Fine," she muttered between clenched teeth.

"I still need help with all those sheets," Rhonda said. "I suppose if everyone is busy, I can just do them myself."

Like that was going to happen, Carly thought. "I'll help," she said. "Tiffany, why don't you write up a draft of what you think is a reasonable chore list and we'll talk about it later this afternoon? Aside from keeping your room clean, you'll need to help around the B and B, so think about what you'd like to do."

"I don't want to be a maid even if it pays good."

"You don't have to be. There are lots of other things. You could help Maribel in the kitchen, you could prepare the evening appetizers, be responsible for arranging the fresh flowers in the public rooms and the guest rooms."

Her daughter perked up. "I don't know how to arrange flowers."

"It's not that hard. I could teach you."

Tiffany's eyes widened. "You know how to do that for real? You were always putting flowers in the house, but I didn't think you really knew what you were doing."

"Gee, thanks for the vote of confidence. My point is there are a lot of ways to help and I don't mind if you pick one that's fun for you."

"Okay. I'll do that." Her expression cleared and she headed out of the room.

Rhonda watched her go. "You're spoiling her."

"Because I'm willing to let her have a say in what her chores are? I don't consider that spoiling, Mom. She's more likely to do the work if she has some input in the process. There's already plenty of friction with her being a teenager. I would like to avoid adding more to the situation."

Her mother shook her head. "I would never have let you pick your chores."

"I know."

Her mother glared at her. "Is that a criticism? Do you want to blame me for the problems in your life? Is it my fault you couldn't hold on to your husband?"

"None of the above," Carly said as she wondered if living in say, Iowa, would really be that bad. "Come on. I'll help you fold the sheets."

She would use the time with her mother to find out the real situation at the B and B and then make her decision about staying or leaving. If she was going to move again, she had to do it soon, before Tiffany got too settled. Plus there was her daughter's school to think of. Spring break was only a week. She didn't want to keep Tiffany out of school because they were moving yet again.

Ten minutes later Carly found herself in the basement laundry room. Despite the fact that it had probably once been a dungeon, the space was bright and airy. Several small windows up by the ceiling let in light while the sunny yellow paint added cheer. Three industrial-size washers lined one wall, and matching dryers lined another. There were long folding tables and cabinets with laundry supplies. A dumbwaiter in the corner allowed the clean laundry to be sent up to the guest floors.

Carly stared at the piles and piles of sheets. They were

on top of the tables, on the machines themselves and in baskets. She could see why her daughter freaked.

"Were you full for the weekend?" she asked her mother as she reached down and pulled out a sheet.

"No. We're a little behind on the laundry."

No kidding, Carly thought. She would guess that laundry hadn't been done in a month.

"This has been hard for you, hasn't it?" Carly said, knowing the conversation would go better if she took her mother's side and was careful not to make anything sound like an accusation. "You've had to take on a lot of responsibility."

Her mother picked up a pillowcase. "It's been horrible. After your father died, I couldn't really function. You can't be married to a man for thirty-five years and just get over it."

"I agree," Carly said.

"At first this place ran itself. I liked being in the familiar surroundings and having all the guests come. The ones who had been returning for years were like old friends. Then business slowed. Just a little at first. But now..."

Her voice trailed off. Carly tried to think of a tactful way to ask how bad it was. Before she could, her mother continued.

"We're still getting the die-hard ghost fanatics. Being in all the registries helps, of course. We *are* the best documented haunted house."

"That's a big plus," Carly said. Without Mary, Chatsworth-by-the-Sea was nothing more than an old English manor in the middle of pretty much nowhere. "But overall, bookings seem to be down."

"I know." Her mother sighed. "People just don't travel the way they used to."

"What kind of advertising are you doing? There are so many specialty magazines and cable channels."

Her mother reached for another pillowcase. "Don't be ridiculous. We can't afford to spend that kind of money on something as silly as advertising."

"It's not silly," Carly told her. "If people don't know the B and B exists, how can they come stay here?"

"They know."

"How? Is there some kind of cosmic information booth that informs them?"

Rhonda pressed her lips together and closed her eyes. "I can't believe, with all I've been through, that you would be so mean to me right now."

Carly stared at her. What, exactly, was making her mother's life so difficult at this exact moment?

"I'm sorry you feel that way," she said, trying to keep her voice even. "I'm trying to point out that people won't know about our place if we don't tell them. Word of mouth is great, but it's a slow way to build up clientele."

She finished with the sheet and set it in a basket. "The thing is, Mom, I need to know how bad things are right now. If I'm going to stay and help you bring the B and B back to a profitable status, I have to know where we're starting from."

"You know we never discuss money in detail. It's rude."

"This is business, Mom. Our family business. I thought you wanted me to help."

"I do."

"Then I need to know what's going on."

Her mother snapped open the pillowcase. "Fine, but I don't want you talking about our personal finances with all your friends."

"I won't." As if she ever had. Ah, but secrets were important in this family.

"Then I'll show you the books. Although I can't imagine what you want with them. You'll never understand them."

Carly gaped at her. "Excuse me? This is what I do for a living. I was in charge of the finances at the doctor's office."

"You don't have to get huffy with me. I thought you had a bookkeeper."

"We did, and I'm the one who checked her work." So much for her mother paying attention when she'd talked about her job, Carly thought in amazement.

"Then I guess you can see them after we finish here," Rhonda said. "Whatever the problems are, they're not my fault."

"Of course not," Carly said automatically.

Whoever said coming home again was a good idea had obviously had a very different family, she thought. Could she do this? Could she work with her mother, live under the same roof, day after day for the next couple of years? Did she want to commit her life to the bed-and-breakfast?

There was still the possibility of a small town somewhere. She could walk away from all of this, let her mother simply sell the old place and get on with her life.

Which choice was better? Which would be the most beneficial for Tiffany? And wouldn't it be great if someone was making decisions with her, Carly's, best interest in mind?

CHAPTER 4

Carly knew the news wasn't going to be good, but she hadn't expected things to be as bad as they were. It took her two hours to study spreadsheets, ledgers and the previous two years of tax returns. She didn't worry about things like payroll or food orders. Instead she focused on guest revenue and large expenditures.

The big surprise was that the B and B had been existing on a line of credit against the home for the past eighteen months. The business hadn't been profitable in nearly three years.

Declining bookings were the real problem. There had been a steady drop since Carly's father had died. The first couple of years after his death showed a slight decline, then the numbers plummeted. The B and B hadn't had a full night since Valentine's weekend, two years ago.

Carly flipped through different ledgers. There wasn't a single wedding or big party planned for the entire summer. No large groups had requested to take over the B and B, something she remembered happening all the time when she'd been growing up.

In addition to the loss of income, there were some interesting choices in the expense department. The dishes had been replaced to the tune of fifty thousand dollars. At the same time, contractors, including their local plumber, hadn't been paid. Based on the checkbook, she had a feeling the property taxes were two months overdue.

Carly leaned back in her chair and studied the pile of books, papers and the blinking cursor on the computer screen. Was it possible to make this work? Could she do it? Making the B and B profitable would mean changing a lot of things, and her mother wasn't a big fan of change. There were—

Her cell phone rang. She reached for it, flipped open the cover and stared at the unfamiliar number.

"Hello," she said after she'd pushed the talk button.

"Hey, Carly. How's it going?"

It wasn't that she didn't recognize the voice—she had lived with the man for over sixteen years. But she wasn't expecting to hear from her ex-husband, and it took a second for her to place him.

"Neil?"

"Hey. What's up?"

She frowned. "Why do you want to know?"

"I'm just being friendly. You know, regular phone chit-chat."

The last two words made her wince. Was there another man on the planet who used "chitchat"?

"Okay. I'm fine, and yourself?"

"Great. I've been looking at boats. Man, there are some beauties out there. I can't really afford anything new, but I've narrowed my choices down to three older sailboats. I can really fix one of them up and then head off to Hawaii. The cost of the navigation system is going to kill me, but it's a pretty big ocean and I sure don't want to get lost."

Uh-huh. Did she get a vote on that? "How nice," she murmured. Was she missing something here? "Neil, why are you calling me?"

"What do you mean?" He sounded genuinely baffled.

"I mean, why are you calling? What is your purpose? Do you want to talk to Tiffany?"

"Naw. I'm just checking in. Saying hi. Hi."

Had she ever thought of the man as charming? "Neil, we're getting a divorce. You decided you didn't want to be with me anymore. So why are you checking in?"

"Because we're friends. Don't you want to be friends with me, Carly?"

Not even for money, she thought. Why didn't Neil get it? She could handle him being as much of a jerk as he wanted where she was concerned, but Tiffany was another matter.

"What I want is for you to stay in contact with your daughter. It's been over three weeks since you last spoke with her."

"I've been busy. This whole boat thing."

"Neil, she's your *daughter*. She has to matter."

"You know you're much better at the whole parenting thing than I am."

What he meant was she was willing to make the sacrifices that went with having a child and he wasn't. "I know she loves you and misses you. Just because you don't have to pay child support while you're not working doesn't mean you abdicate your responsibilities. You're supposed to see her every other weekend. She needs that and I think you need the time with her, too. She's growing up fast. You have to be a part of her life."

"Lighten up. You take things too seriously."

Carly held the phone out in front of her and stared at it. She replaced it against her ear. "You're kidding, right? We're talking about your *child*."

"I know."

His tone dismissed her in such a way that in less than three seconds she went from annoyed to wanting to maim him.

How did this always happen? They started out with her wanting him to change something and they ended up with her being the bad guy. She wanted to scream at him that it had never been her plan to take life so seriously, but no one had given her much of a choice. Someone had needed to be the grown-up and Neil sure as hell hadn't volunteered. It had all fallen on her.

"You know, Carly, if you're going to be like this, I'm not going to call you anymore."

"Amazingly enough, I can live with that. The person you need to be calling is Tiffany. You need to plan to spend a weekend with her and soon. I mean it, Neil. If you don't do this in the next two weeks, I'm contacting the judge. I'll make it a court order if I have to."

Tiffany adored her father and Carly was going to make sure the man didn't let her little girl down any more than he already had.

He grumbled something she couldn't hear but doubted was very flattering to her.

"Fine. But what about the plane ticket? Do I have to pay to fly her down?"

"Yes. Or you could come up here, but you're not staying at the B and B. You'll have to get two hotel rooms somewhere else. And before you ask, yes, Tiffany needs her own room. She's fifteen."

"But that's a lot of money."

"So sail up here on your boat. That will be free."

"What? Hey, Carly, that's a great idea. Maybe I'll do that."

"So there's no point in telling you I was being sarcastic about the sailing remark?"

"Naw. Okay. Gotta run. Have a good one."

He hung up.

She did a little grumbling herself, then pushed the end button on her cell phone.

What on earth made Neil think she wanted to be friends with him? Sure, she was more than willing to keep things civil between them. It was important for them to get along—for Tiffany's sake. But friends?

Maybe she would be a better person if she were willing to let Neil stay in her life, but that was *so* not her style. She'd moved past wanting to see him cut up into little pieces and fed to the carnivores at the L.A. zoo, but that didn't mean she wanted to "chitchat" about his hopes and dreams.

None of which mattered, she reminded herself. What

was important was his relationship with his daughter. If he followed through on that, she would ignore the rest of it. If he didn't, she would make good on her threat to get in touch with the judge.

In the meantime, she had books to put in order and a profit-and-loss statement to work out.

But instead of reaching for the keyboard and entering numbers on the spreadsheet, she turned her chair toward the office window and stared out over the side lawn.

What had happened to chase guests away? Or had they simply forgotten about the B and B? Was it the same with the groups and the weddings? Carly remembered attending large bridal fairs with her parents at least twice a year. Then there were a couple of big travel shows. There had been brochures and pictures and letters of recommendation by previous guests.

Without turning away from the window, she reached for a notepad and a pen.

"Contact previous guests by postcard, giving them a discount," she wrote. They still had the old registration information. Sure, the mailing would be expensive, but they would be reaching people who had wanted to come at one time.

What next? Weddings, parties of all kinds. They were

coming into the busy season. If she spoke with some of the local hotels in town, told them they had availability, maybe they could get some spillover bookings.

They could run specials during the slow seasons and they weren't that far from San Francisco. What about advertising locally? Chatsworth-by-the-Sea was off the beaten path, but they did have a ghost. She would have to feature that prominently.

Okay, those ideas worked for the weekends, but what about during the week? Based on what she'd discovered, the place was mostly empty, even on holiday weeks. So what made people travel during the week, when most of them were working? What would make them give up their precious vacation time to come here? Or was she missing the point? What if they got to come here without giving up vacation time? What if their travel was about work?

Carly grinned as she put pen to paper and began to write as fast as she could form words.

"This is just stupid," Tiffany said from the passenger seat. "I don't want to go to school."

Carly resisted the urge to remind her daughter that she loved school. The classes were mildly interesting, but what really got Tiffany excited was the activities and hanging out with her friends. No doubt if she said that, she would be reminded that due to the move, Tiffany had no friends locally.

"Even if I wanted to let you stay home, which I don't," she said, "the state of California has a real thing about truancy. You gotta be there, kid."

"But I'll hate it. Besides, Grandma said she's not sure we're staying, so why don't I wait until you decide what you want to do about ruining my life even more?"

Carly stared at her daughter. "What?"

Tiffany sighed. "Grandma said we may not be staying with her. That you've mentioned going somewhere else. Not that you'd discuss it with me. I'm just the one with the broken life. Why should I know anything?"

Carly felt her temper rise and it had nothing to do with Tiffany's negative attitude. How dare her mother discuss moving with Tiffany? Carly hadn't decided what to do about staying or leaving, but she'd been determined not to worry Tiffany until she had a clearer plan. Tiffany was only fifteen—her life should be about classes and friends and boys and growing up. Not worrying about where they were going to live.

"I'm sorry Grandma said anything," Carly told her. "It's true I don't know if we're staying. I've been working on trying to figure out if I think I can make the bed-and-breakfast profitable. She and I are going to talk about my plan this afternoon. I've come up with some ideas and suggestions, but ultimately, it's her decision whether or not she wants to keep the place open. If she doesn't, then we'll be moving somewhere else. But until we know otherwise, we're assuming we're staying."

"Easy for you to say. Your life isn't destroyed."

Tiffany folded her arms over her chest and stared out the window. Hard to believe this was the same girl who had, only a few nights earlier, wanted to sleep in her mother's bed. She'd worried that Tiffany was growing up so fast. Maybe she should worry she wasn't growing up fast enough.

"I'm working through the last of the numbers this morning, then I have to talk to your grandmother. As soon as we know, you'll know."

Tiffany didn't say anything, but her folded arms and closed expression more than communicated her displeasure. Carly knew it was going to get a whole lot worse with her daughter before it got better. Tiffany had never changed schools before, and while Carly wanted to believe the transition would be smooth, she had her doubts.

Funny how knowing a situation had the potential to be difficult didn't make it any more pleasant when it occurred.

She pulled up in front of the high school and stared at

the familiar building. Wings had been added on each end, nearly doubling it in size, but even with the addition and the two separate buildings behind the main one, it was still much smaller than the school Tiffany had attended in Santa Monica.

"This is it?" the teen asked in disbelief. "What are there, like twelve students?"

"I'm sure there are at least twenty," Carly said as she turned off the car and unfastened her seat belt. "Come on. Let's get you registered. I called last week and the office already had your transcripts, so that will help."

"Nothing's going to help," Tiffany muttered.

Carly ignored that and walked toward the main entrance. She remembered everything about this school—she'd attended it herself. More years ago than she could count, she'd been thrilled to finally be in high school. It had seemed so mature and exciting. Some of the seniors had been close to eighteen. The senior guys all had deep voices and a lot had beards or mustaches.

Carly smiled as she recalled clinging to Maribel as both of them had stared at all the older guys. It had been like waking up on a different planet—an exciting one filled with possibilities. She and her friend had spent that first lunch period walking around the campus, figuring out where things were. One of the seniors had actually smiled at them and said hi. Carly had a feeling she and Maribel had shrieked and run off in the opposite direction.

Hard to believe she'd ever been that innocent and silly. Good times, she thought wryly.

She led the way to the administration desk. None of the staff looked familiar, which made sense. She'd been out of high school nearly…

Carly did the math, redid it, then groaned. Nearly twenty-two years. Was that possible? No way. She wasn't *that* old, was she? Apparently she was. Talk about depressing.

"May I help you?" the young woman behind the desk asked as Carly leaned against the counter.

"I'm here to register my daughter. Her transcripts were sent ahead. I called last week to confirm."

The woman smiled. "Of course. Tiffany Spencer."

Tiffany shuffled up to the counter and gave the heavy sigh of a child being punished by horrible parents.

"I'm new," she said with as much cheerfulness as those facing certain death in the Spanish Inquisition.

"I know settling in to a new school can be difficult, but you'll do fine, honey," the woman said. "I'm Jenny. I work here in the office. Let me get your file and we'll figure out what classes you're taking. Oh, and you'll want to meet with Mrs. Beecham, the girls' vice principal. Just this one time," Jenny added with a wink. "You don't want to make a habit of hanging out with her."

Jenny bustled out of the front office and disappeared into a rear room. Carly looked at her daughter.

"She seems nice."

"Sure. And lame. We're not going to be friends. Why does she want to pretend any of this matters?"

"Can't she just be a nice person who wants to help?"

"Right. Plus it's totally weird that you went here. It was a really long time ago, but still. What if one of the teachers remembers you? I don't want anyone talking about that. Then I won't make any friends for sure."

Carly thought about pointing out that most of the kids in the school were locals and most likely their parents had attended the school, as well, but she doubted Tiffany would find any comfort in that.

"A lot of my teachers were pretty old," she said instead. "I'm guessing many of them are retired."

There were a few exceptions. Her gym teacher had been in her twenties and Mr. Everwood, her math teacher, had just finished college. Carly almost mentioned that when she remembered how both she and Maribel had had huge crushes on the man. He'd been maybe twenty-five and very hunky, in an older man sort of way.

She and Maribel had sat together in his geometry and algebra classes, giggling softly at the wonder of being so close to the object of their affection. Mr. Everwood had broken their hearts their second year when he'd invited them to his wedding.

Maribel had been out of town that weekend, but Carly had bravely attended with a couple of other friends. She'd found her heart miraculously mended when a junior on the basketball team, also a student of Mr. Everwood's, had danced with her twice, then asked her out for the following Saturday.

"What's so funny?" Tiffany asked suspiciously. "You're smiling. It's because you're thinking of a new way to make me miserable, aren't you?"

Carly laughed. "Not even a little. I'll tell you a secret, Tiffany. Not everything in the world is about you."

"I know. Just the bad stuff is."

Thirty minutes later Tiffany had a class schedule, books, a locker and was being led away by the ever-cheerful and pleasant Jenny. Carly turned from the administration office and walked back toward the main entrance. As she reached for the door handle to head to her car, someone called her name.

"Carly? Carly Washington?"

Carly stopped, turned and blinked at the tall man walking toward her. He was familiar. Older, sure, with gray at his temples. He wore his dark hair shorter, and there were more lines than she remembered. The brightly printed shirts he'd favored had been replaced with solid-color ones, and he'd probably put on ten or fifteen pounds. Otherwise, he was exactly the same.

"Mr. Everwood," she said, feeling herself blush even though she knew there was no way he could have a clue that she'd been thinking about him a few minutes before. "Wow. You're still here."

He grinned as he approached. "I know. I should have gone on to bigger and better things, but I love teaching. I've tried not to, but I think it's too late for me to change now." He stared into her eyes. His were still dark brown.

"But that's great. We need good teachers and you were that. I'm sure you still are."

"I like to think so. You wouldn't recognize the old classroom. These days we do a lot with computers and programming. Every student has a computer station in nearly all the classes."

"That will make Tiffany happy. She's of that generation—the one that doesn't remember a world without computers."

Carly nearly groaned. Could this conversation be more lame? Could *she?*

"How old is your daughter?"

"Fifteen."

"She might be in my class."

"I hope not," Carly said, trying to relax. "She's deathly afraid of coming face-to-face with one of my old, um, former teachers and have him or her tell the class I used to go here. So if she is in your class I would appreciate you not saying anything. Lucky for me, I didn't mention I'd ever had Mr. Everwood for math."

He raised his eyebrows. "We're both adults, Carly. You can call me Steve now."

Steve? Steve? No. That wasn't going to happen. She'd been raised to call teachers by their last names and there was no way she could ever think of Mr. Everwood as anything but a teacher. Steve?

"Okay. Sure."

The humor faded from his eyes. "I sometimes speak with your mother," he said. "I'm sorry to hear about your divorce."

News sure spread fast, she thought, knowing she shouldn't be surprised. "Thanks. I'm okay with it."

"I'm glad to hear that. Of course your husband's stupidity is my gain."

Carly knew her mouth was open because she'd felt her jaw drop. Was Mr. Everwood coming on to her?

"Yes, well, at least we've managed to stay on speaking terms." She swallowed. "Me and my ex-husband. Not you and me. Of course we can speak, too."

"I'd like that."

He would? Why?

"Okay. Great. Look, I really have to get back to the B and B."

"Sure. Would you mind if I gave you a call sometime?"

Him? Call her? For what?

She wanted to run shrieking into the night, except it was day and shrieking would only make her look stupid.

"That would be fine," she said as she backed toward the door. "You probably have the number."

"Of course. Good to see you, Carly."

"You, too, Mr., um, Steve."

Carly drove directly to the B and B, then breathed a sigh of relief when she saw Maribel's car still parked in the side lot. She flew across the gravel and raced into the kitchen.

"Where's my mom?" she asked Maribel, who had just put a bowl into the refrigerator.

"Upstairs. Why? Is something wrong? Were you in an accident?"

"What? No. Oh, God." Carly pulled out a stool and sank down, then she looked at her friend and started to laugh. "I registered Carly for school," she said, between bursts of laughter.

"Sounds like it was a fun experience."

"It was fine, but afterward I ran into Mr. Everwood."

Maribel sat next to her and patted her arm. "We're all adults now, Carly. It's okay to call him Steve."

"That's what he said," Carly told her even as she lost control of another burst of giggles. "I think he asked me out. He said he was going to call. Mr. Everwood. Twenty-three years ago I would have been thrilled, but now it's just plain weird. Besides, isn't he married?"

"A widower, and something of a ladies' man. You be careful around him."

Carly held in another shriek. "Our former math teacher is a ladies' man? I can't grasp the concept. And you don't have to worry about me. I'm not going out with him. There's a huge *ick* factor. This guy used to be my teacher."

"Twenty years ago."

"I know, but still. I can barely call him Steve. I certainly can't date him."

Dating? Not in this lifetime. Or at least not for a very long time. She already had too much going on.

"I'm still trying to get settled here. Plus, I was married for nearly seventeen years. The last thing I'm looking for is another man."

"What about sex?" Maribel asked with a grin.

Carly stared at her. "You can't expect me to have sex with Mr. Everwood!"

"I guess not if you can't call him by his first name. He's actually pretty nice and not bad looking. I'm just saying be careful. He has a reputation for being a love 'em and leave 'em kind of guy."

"This is too surreal," Carly said. "Tell me it's five o'clock somewhere. I think I need wine."

Instead of drowning her sorrows in a glass of chardonnay, Carly chose to put her morning activities behind her and work on her plan. She'd decided to make a formal presentation to her mother, putting everything in writing so they were both clear on where they were going. Assuming this all came to pass.

After spending most of the past four days brainstorming ways to bring the inn back to profitable status, she found herself getting more and more excited about the possibilities. If her mother agreed with Carly's ideas, there was a better-than-even chance they could make a lot of money. Things had a chance of going badly, as well, but Carly didn't want to think about that.

She ran the numbers for the fourth time that afternoon, then made sure all her spreadsheets were in order. While she would have liked to do her presentation on the computer, she thought her mother would be more comfortable with actual paper in front of her.

She was so engrossed in what she was doing that she didn't notice the time, and was shocked when Tiffany stormed into her room.

"I'll never forgive you," the teen announced as tears spilled down her face. "Never, ever."

Carly glanced at the clock and was surprised to see it was nearly three-thirty. She was supposed to meet with her mother at four.

She put aside her paper and rose to face her daughter. Obviously her first day at a new high school hadn't been a success.

"Tell me what happened," Carly said quietly.

"Nothing. Exactly nothing. No one talked to me, no one even looked at me. It's like I was invisible. I sat by myself at lunch. That's *never* happened to me before. I'm the popular one. I'm the one who gets to say who's in and who isn't."

She wiped her face, then threw her books on the bed. "Plus you let Grandma come pick me up. Do you know how humiliating that was? She was standing outside the car! She called my name and waved."

Carly winced. When her mother had offered to pick up Tiffany, Carly had been grateful for the extra time to polish her work. She hadn't thought to warn her not to acknowledge Tiffany in any way until she was in the car and they were safely out of sight of her friends.

"I'm sorry about that," Carly told her. "I know this seems horrible now, but it will get better."

"How do you know?" Tiffany demanded. "You never changed schools when you were growing up. You never had your life destroyed. I hate you! This is all your f-fault." Her voice broke on a sob. "If you weren't such a bitch, Daddy never would have left us. We wouldn't have had to move here. *You* did this. You—"

Her eyes widened and her mouth opened, as if she'd just realized what she'd said.

Carly experienced her own brand of shock. Her daughter had gotten angry with her before—countless times—but she'd never sworn at her. Sympathy turned to annoyance and threatened to grow into something else.

She wanted a chance to have her own tantrum. When did she get to rage at the unfairness of it all? She wanted to give her daughter a few facts about where the blame lay, and point out that her precious father had only called under threat of a court order.

Then the anger grew and was joined by the sharp pain of raising a teenager and being the bad guy all the time. Eventually she and Tiffany would reconnect. Eventually her daughter would understand what was important, but that era of peace and unity was years away. Until then there was only this.

"I meant it," Tiffany said, raising her chin. "I don't care if you punish me. What does it matter if I'm grounded? I don't have anywhere to go or anyone to see."

Carly turned away. "Get out of here."

"What? Aren't you going to punish me?"

"Right now I don't even want to look at you. Go to your room and stay there."

"You can't tell me what to do."

Carly turned on her daughter. She didn't raise her voice,

but for once she didn't hide her disappointment, anger and pain.

"Get out of my sight."

Tiffany gasped, grabbed her books and fled.

CHAPTER 5

Carly did her best to clear Tiffany from her mind as she set out the papers in front of her mother. A couple of hours alone in her room might give the teen time to rethink her words and actions and come to the conclusion that she'd been rude and wrong. Given Tiffany's current hormone level and mental state, it seemed unlikely; but hey, a mom could dream.

"I'm interested in a three-pronged approach to growing our bottom line," Carly said after she'd set up an easel and put up the first graphic of three arrows pointing up. "First, individual bookings, second, group bookings and third, day visitors. The individual bookings are going to account for most of our weekend reservations, so the other two need to fill up our midweek slots. My marketing emphasis will be based on the haunted-house angle. It's the only way we'll get people to come out here. The decrease in visitors in recent years proves that without a hook, we're not going to make it."

She flipped to the second graphic, this one showing a couple in a car. "I want to use the existing database to send out a letter to all our previous customers. We can offer them a twenty-percent discount for their next stay. I'll also put together some packages—a cooking weekend, day trips to Napa, or an afternoon on a marine research vessel. I already have some contacts there."

Her mother didn't comment, nor could Carly read her expression. So she just kept on talking.

"We'll advertise in very specific magazines. I've listed them on page two, along with their rates."

Her mother flipped the page. "This is a lot of money," Rhonda told her.

Carly thought about pointing out it was way less than it had cost to replace perfectly good china and flatware, but didn't.

"I have more specifics on attracting couples and families, but right now I'd like to continue the overview," she said. "The group bookings would be small conferences. There are lots of groups looking for a unique place to come and have a two- or three-day session. I've had interest from some horror writers—obviously they're excited about the ghost angle. There are three culinary institutes who would like to book for three- and five-day sessions at a haunted house. Management off-sites are another opportunity. I'm still getting information on that."

"This is all very nice, Carly, but I don't want a bunch of strangers in my house."

Carly opened her mouth, then closed it. "Mom, this is a bed-and-breakfast. Strangers is what we do."

Her mother sighed. "You know what I mean. Nice married couples are one thing, but horror writers? And I don't want a bunch of business people here."

Carly had expected resistance, but not like this. "What do you have against business people?"

"For one thing, we only offer breakfast. I'm not interested in opening a restaurant."

"I agree. It's too expensive and too iffy. But we can offer boxed lunches with advance notice, and catering. I've spoken to several of the restaurants in town and they're more than willing to deliver out here. In fact, the boxed lunches tie in with my idea for day visitors. We could offer the larger, public rooms for meetings of local clubs. Civic groups, women's groups. We make a couple of bucks a head on their lunch and give them the parlors for free."

"How is that going to help anything?"

"If they like what they see then they'll think about holding their daughter's wedding here. Or a birthday party. Or putting up out-of-town guests. We need to remind the world we're still here. I've spoken with a few groups and they're very interested. They love the idea that we're haunted."

"Seems like you've been talking to the world."

"Just trying to get a handle on things. Everyone who has been here loves the place and those who haven't are really intrigued. Without the ghost angle, I couldn't get anyone to return calls. But Mary is a fabulous selling point. Who wouldn't want to stay at a haunted B and B? That's going to be our main selling point with the management off-sites. That, and the quiet."

Rhonda flipped through the pages. "I just don't know. It's all so much. Do we have to do this?"

Carly sat across from her. "No, we don't. But if you don't want to make changes then you need to sell right now. The B and B is losing between two and three thousand dollars a month just to stay running and that doesn't count the repairs or any replacement costs. Or property taxes. They're incredibly high. At the rate you're burning through the equity in this place, you have about three years left."

"What happens in three years?"

"You won't be able to get enough money out of the sale to live on the proceeds. You'll have to get a job."

Rhonda leaned back in her chair. "I don't want that. I'm ready to retire."

"I know, Mom. The thing is, I would really hate for you to sell this house after all this time. It's a part of our heritage. But I also want you to be financially secure. What I propose is that you give me one year to get the B and B back on its feet financially. If I can't do it, then you can still sell and have your nest egg. If I can, then we'll go back to what we'd always talked about—that I would take over the business and slowly buy you out."

"You want to make a lot of changes. I'm not comfortable with this. Why does it have to be different?"

"Because you're losing a lot of money."

Her mother closed her eyes. "I hate this. I wish your father hadn't died. He always took care of everything. This has been so hard for me."

Carly sat next to her and took her hand. "It has. It's been a long seven years and you've done a great job. But I don't want you to lose your retirement and I really don't want to lose the house."

Rhonda nodded, then looked at her daughter. "I just don't know if you can do it. What if you fail?"

Carly tried not to take the lack of confidence personally. "I'm asking for a year. That's all. If things aren't going well at the end of that time, you can still sell and get out enough to live on for the rest of your life."

"All right. I'll think about it."

Carly held in a sigh. Her mother was notorious for thinking about things for weeks at a time and then still not deciding.

"I need to know by tomorrow."

"What?" Her mother glared at her. "I can't decide something this big that quickly. You're pressuring me. What does it matter if I take a few weeks?"

"It matters to me. I need Tiffany settled. If you're going to say no, I need to find a job somewhere else and get her into a new school. I don't want to have her start to make friends here only to uproot her again. It's not fair. I'm asking you to decide in a reasonable time frame. I have responsibilities to my daughter, and I take them as seriously as you took your responsibilities to me."

Her mother's eyes filled with tears. "This isn't fair. If your father were still alive…"

"But he isn't."

"You think I don't know that? I've had to deal with this all by myself. You haven't been any help. You've been running around having a good time while I suffered."

Carly stood and stepped back a couple of steps. "I've been raising my child."

"With that no-good man you married. I don't understand it. And now you come back here and want to order me around."

Carly knew that however this went, she was going to be the bad guy. "That's not my intent. I saw us as partners. I've offered my vision for what we can do to make the B and B successful again. I'm willing to work sixteen-hour days and devote myself to the project. All I ask in return is for you to either agree or disagree. But I won't wait forever. If you don't like what I want to do, then you'll need time to figure out what you want to do instead."

"Oh, sure. Put it all on me. You've always been difficult, but I don't remember you being so hard-hearted. When did that happen?"

"I have no idea," Carly told her, feeling both sad and resigned. Why couldn't her mother simply make a decision? Obviously she'd known changes would have to happen to make the business a success.

Of course Carly already knew the answer to that. If her mother decided anything, then she had to take responsibility—the one thing she hated to do. Life was better when whatever went wrong was someone else's fault.

"You're not giving me much choice," Rhonda said. "Either I agree or you walk away from me forever."

"That's not what I said. If the B and B is going to be closed, then I have to make a life for myself and my daughter. That's hardly abandoning you."

Rhonda didn't look convinced. "Fine. Have it your way. You'd probably do it without me."

Carly sank back into the chair. "You're saying yes? You're agreeing with my plan?"

"Yes. It's your idea and you're in charge."

Carly understood the momspeak. That she wasn't just in charge, she was responsible. If anything went wrong, she was to blame.

She was okay with that—in this case it was true.

"I suppose you'll be taking over everything," her mother said sadly. "I won't matter at all."

"That's not true. I'll need your help more than ever. With me getting all the advertising in place and coming up with different ideas, I'll be swamped. You're the heart and soul of this B and B, Mom. You always have been. Yes, I have a lot of things I want to get done, but none of it will happen without you."

She squeezed her mother's hand. "I mean that."

At that moment Rhonda looked old and small. Carly opened her mouth, then closed it.

Was that the *real* problem? That her mother didn't feel needed by anyone?

Rhonda sighed. "I just don't have the energy I used to, but if you need me, of course I'll be there."

"Thanks. I want to take the load off you and I will. But at first I'll need your help in the day-to-day running of things. At least until I'm up to speed and can do some re-arranging of the staff."

"All right," Rhonda said. "We'll be a team."

"Great." Carly smiled. "I'm going to do everything I can to make the B and B a success."

"I hope it works," Rhonda said. "If it doesn't, we'll all know you tried your best and that's what matters."

Carly accepted the words in the spirit they were given—or at least in the spirit she wanted them to be given. She leaned forward and hugged her mother. The soft scent of Chanel No. 5 surrounded her.

"You'll see," she said. "It's going to be great."

And it would be. Just as soon as Carly stopped the money hemorrhage, got a few more guests and figured out what she was going to do with her daughter. Then it would be great.

Her small moment of celebration lasted for as long as it took to climb to her daughter's room. After a quick knock, she stepped inside. The bedroom was empty, but she heard a chair squeak in the small parlor.

Carly didn't want to have this conversation. She wanted things to be as they had been two or three years ago. Before her daughter had become so difficult and demanding. Sure, it was just a teenage thing, but why did she have to suffer, too?

Squaring her shoulders, she crossed the floor and entered the second room. Tiffany sat in a chair by the window. She didn't look up as Carly entered.

"It's not my fault," the teen said before Carly could speak. "You're messing everything up and I'm reacting to that. If we'd stayed back in Santa Monica, none of this would have happened."

Carly didn't know what to address first—the obvious lie that if they hadn't moved Tiffany would have behaved perfectly, or the complete lack of responsibility.

"So this is my fault?" she asked incredulously.

"Yes." Her daughter glared at her. "You're making me act this way."

The words were different, but the intent was the same. Painfully the same, and familiar. It took Carly a second to place it and when she did, she didn't know if she should laugh or cry.

"Oh, my God. You're exactly like my mother," Carly said in horror. "You don't take responsibility for anything and you're completely selfish."

"What?" Tiffany yelped. "That's not true."

Carly barely heard her. She pulled out the desk chair and sat down. Her brain seemed to be swelling by the second. Was it true? Was it possible?

"You're exactly like her," she repeated, more to herself than to Tiffany. "You blame me for your actions, you can't see any view but your own. How did this happen? Did I do it? Did I grow up a certain way based on my mother? Did my hyper sense of responsibility mean you didn't have to be responsible for anything?"

Had she screwed up her daughter as much as she'd been screwed up herself? Was this the legacy she had inadvertently passed on?

"Is it just your age?" Carly asked. "Or is it your character?"

Tiffany stood and waved her arms. "Hello. Still in the room. Stop talking about me as if I'm not here."

"What? Oh. Right." Carly looked at her daughter. "Because this is all about you."

Tiffany stomped her foot. "Stop saying that. I'm not selfish."

"And the last time you thought about anyone was when? You accused me of ruining things so your father left. Here's a news flash—it takes two to make or break a marriage. I'm willing to accept my responsibility in what went wrong, but your father has his, as well. We were equal partners in what happened. You can continue to blame me, but that doesn't change the truth. As for what you did—there's no excuse. You hurt me because you don't care about me. I'm working my butt off to make your life better and all you can see is what's wrong with it."

She rose. This revelation about her daughter deserved some serious thought. If she was contributing to Tiffany's center-of-the-universe thinking, she was going to have to change how she interacted with her daughter. She headed for the door.

"Wait," Tiffany called. "What about me?"

Carly turned and stared at her. "What about you?"

"Aren't you going to punish me? For what I said." Tiffany looked both angry and afraid.

"Will that make you feel better?" Carly asked. "Will that take away some of the guilt?"

Her daughter nodded.

"Then not just yet."

Carly returned to her room and started to organize the papers on her desk. First up, she needed her own office.

There were several available spaces downstairs. She would clear one out and move her stuff in.

Thank goodness her laptop was relatively new. She wouldn't have to buy a new computer anytime soon. She could—

She set down the folder she'd grabbed and leaned back in her chair. She was really going to do this. Her! She was going to turn this business around and make it a success. Whatever happened, wherever they ended up, it would be because of her hard work, her ideas, her vision. No one was making her do this and no one was offering advice. It was totally and completely up to her.

The idea of being that much in charge was both terrifying and freeing. Sure, if she failed it was public, big-time, and had a huge impact on many lives. But if she didn't… If it worked, then it was something she could point to with pride.

The need to share the slightly thrilling, slightly scary moment had her reaching for the phone. But who would she call? Maribel was busy with her family, and all her L.A. friends had turned out to be less than friendly.

"I wish you were here, Mary," she murmured aloud, but the ghost didn't appear. Not that she actually expected her to. Ghosts weren't real, right? Except Carly needed the ghost. Having a haunted B and B had opened doors for her.

Without a "shimmering essence," she was unlikely to turn the business around.

A problem to deal with later. Right now she could celebrate her pending business venture with a trip downstairs to pick out her office. She could move in that afternoon, then come up with a schedule. In a perfect world, she would spend mornings working on growing the business and afternoons learning all the ins and outs of the B and B. Not that her life was going to be that tidy, but still, she could dream.

She stood to head out when someone knocked on her bedroom door. As the person on the other side was likely to be either her mother or daughter, she briefly thought about pretending to be somewhere else.

But in the end she sighed, then called, "It's open."

Tiffany stepped into her room. Her eyes were red and swollen and her lower lip trembled.

Carly had always considered herself a soft touch. Still, she didn't say anything. Maybe being a soft touch had contributed to her daughter's lack of responsibility.

"Yes?" Carly asked.

Tiffany flinched. "I'm sorry."

Carly waited. Right now those two words weren't good enough.

Tiffany swallowed. "I'm sorry I called you a bad word. I shouldn't have done it. I was mad."

"You hurt me. I love you more than anyone in the world. I would die for you. I know you're going through a lot and it's unreasonable to expect you to completely understand I'm going through some things, too, but you have to learn that you can't always blurt out what you're thinking. There are consequences for words and actions."

Tiffany began to cry. "Do you hate me?"

"I've never hated you. Sometimes I don't like you very much."

Her daughter seemed genuinely shocked. "But you're my mom."

"I know that. I love you. I always will. But liking you is different."

"B-but you have to like me." Tears spilled down her cheeks. "I'm sorry, Mom. I'm really, really sorry. I know I can be a brat and I'll try really hard to do better. I just get so mad and it gets big inside."

And Carly was a safe target. She opened her arms. Tiffany threw herself into them and held on tight.

"I'm sorry," she repeated.

Carly stroked her hair. "I accept your apology."

Tiffany sniffed. "Really? You're going to punish me now?"

"Absolutely."

"Oh, good."

Carly smiled at that. "Whoever thought you'd be happy with the idea of being punished?"

"Yeah. Don't tell anyone. So what's it going to be?"

"All the wood furniture in the public rooms need to be polished."

Tiffany stepped back. "There's a ton."

"Probably closer to two tons. You'll have a week to get it all done. After dinner I'll show you where the supplies are and how to do it."

"Okay."

Now that the ugly stuff was out of the way, Carly wanted to share the rest of her news. "Grandma agreed to my plan. We're going to stay here and make the B and B work."

"Really." Tiffany sounded more cautious than excited. "And that's good?"

"I think so. I know you're hating school right now, but you'd have to start over anywhere we went. At least it's pretty here, and we have a cool house. You'll make friends. Imagine the slumber parties you could have here."

Tiffany brightened at the thought. "That would be good. Maybe a real party. You know, with boys."

"Hmm, maybe not for another year or so."

"Oh, Mom."

"Yeah, yeah, I know. I'm a serious drag. But here's the good part. I'm going to be doing a lot of advertising for the B and B. I want your help on that. You can design the graphics and work on the ads. That sort of thing. It will be your chore. We'll work out a schedule, and if you're spending more time on it than we decide, I'll pay you."

"Really? That's so cool."

"I'm glad you think so."

Some might question her decision to seek input from a fifteen-year-old, but Tiffany had inherited all of Neil's marketing sense and was a whiz on the computer.

"There's a great computer lab at school," Tiffany said. "Maybe I can hang out there at lunch and do some work on this. It's not like I have anyone to talk to."

"I appreciate your cooperation," Carly said, ignoring the dig about school. She knew that would get better fairly quickly. "This is going to be fun. And when you're grown up, you'll love having this place as part of your history."

"I'll inherit it, right?" her ever-thoughtful, ever-sensitive daughter asked. "When you're dead, I mean? Then I can sell it and use the money to buy a really great car."

"I'm sure none of us can wait."

CHAPTER 6

Carly typed on the keyboard and then pushed the enter button. The numbers on the computer screen wiggled and danced, then quickly rearranged into a simple profit-and-loss statement. She studied the bottom line and grimaced. Bad. They were still hemorrhaging money, but at least doing so was helping them achieve something.

"Is this a good time?"

She looked up and saw Maribel standing in the entrance to her office.

"Absolutely." Carly saved the file, then turned toward her friend. "The whole numbers thing makes me crazy. Some days I know I can do it and others I just want to run screaming into the mist, never to be heard from again."

Maribel sank onto the chair next to Carly's desk and

handed her a file. Then she reached around and began to rub the small of her back.

"It's only been three weeks," her friend reminded her. "Give yourself a break. You've already made a ton of changes."

"Thanks. How are you feeling?"

"Seriously pregnant. I'm reaching the stage where everything hurts."

"You can stop working anytime," Carly reminded her. "Your daughter has graciously agreed to fill in for you while she's on summer break from college."

"That's because I didn't raise a fool," Maribel said with a smile. "Lisa has figured out she can make more working for you *and* be done with her workday by eleven in the morning. That leaves her plenty of time to hang out with her friends." Maribel leaned back in the chair and rested a hand on her belly. "I've given her all the recipes and I'll be just a phone call away."

"I'm not concerned," Carly told her. "We'll be fine."

"I know. It's just I feel bad missing out on all the fun. After years of the same old same old, new things are happening. Oh, speaking of which, here are the menus I worked up. Your idea for box lunches from town is a good one, but we can definitely make them cheaper ourselves. Even with a part-time person devoted to them, we come out ahead."

Carly flipped through the pages her friend had brought. Although she'd contacted a deli in town to provide box lunches, she'd wondered about having them made on-site. It gave her a little more flexibility, although it added to her stress level by giving her another thing to worry about.

"What do you think?" she asked.

Maribel grinned. "Wow. Someone wants my opinion on more than the location of the soccer ball or a backpack. I'm flattered."

Carly chuckled. "I know that one. But I mean it. I don't think I'd start this up until you were ready to come back to work. I'd need your help. Are you willing to take on supervising a helper?"

"Ooh, management. Sure. I could handle that. I wouldn't mind putting in a few extra hours a week."

"Good. I'll go over your numbers and figure out what I want to do," Carly said. "I'm leaning toward moving our sandwich operations here."

"If you do, I have a couple of cookie recipes I want to try. I've been playing around with them and if I can get them the way I want them, we could include them in the lunches." Maribel tucked her hair behind her ears and cleared her throat. "Okay, it's more than that. I've been thinking maybe we could go in on the cookie thing together. Sell them here under a special Chatsworth-by-the-Sea label. Split the profits."

"I like it," Carly said. "We could have them in the guests' rooms when they arrive, then sell them. We could get into some kind of limited mail order. Of course not right now. I'm not sure I can deal with one more thing."

"Right back at you," Maribel said. "But let's talk about it again after the baby."

Carly flipped forward a few months on her calendar and wrote "cookies." "Think I'll know what that means?"

"Hope so. I'll remember even if you don't." Her friend touched her arm. "Are you doing okay?"

"Yeah. I am. It's insane. When my mom agreed to all this, I told her I'd be working sixteen-hour days, and I wasn't kidding. There's a lot of work. But I'm pulling it together."

Carly pointed to a binder on her desk. "Those are menus from local restaurants willing to deliver. I have a two-day seminar next week and local civic groups lined up. The model-airplane club booked every room for the long weekend in ten days. And there is a group of horror writers coming here for a retreat at the end of June."

Maribel grinned. "Horror writers?"

"It's the ghost thing. I guess they think they'll be inspired. In fact all of our guests, except the model-plane guys, are here because of Mary. I just wish she'd make an appearance."

"Sort of a personal haunting?"

"Yeah. I haven't seen any sign of her since I've been back."

"I've *never* seen her," Maribel said with a laugh. "Remember? You saw her all the time when we were kids. I just felt a chilly brush and tried not to feel slighted that it wasn't more."

Carly tried not to ignore the fact that she was wishing for the moon. "Having a ghost in residence is a huge selling point. That appealing fact is responsible for most of our new bookings. But a ghost? For real?"

Maribel shrugged. "You used to believe."

"Then I grew up. But I would swear I saw something. I know I felt it."

"You and me both. Maybe you should go on the Internet and see if there's a way to lure a spirit here. You don't specifically need Mary. Pretty much any spirit would do." Maribel laughed. "I can't believe I just said that."

"It *is* crazy."

"But you'll go investigate?"

Carly nodded. "A ghost would be cool. But a friendly one."

"Right. Maybe you could take applications."

The two women laughed together.

"But do me a favor," Maribel said. "Wait until I'm out of here to try anything. I'm not really ghost-friendly."

"Fair enough."

Carly glanced around the large office she'd made for herself. After painting the walls a pale yellow, she'd moved in an old desk, a large table for additional workspace and a couple of bookcases. Next door was a conference room she'd decorated with comfortable chairs from the attic.

"I'm really doing this," she said, both pleased and stunned by the way things were working out.

"You're not just doing it, you're doing it well." Maribel glanced at the open door and leaned close. "A couple of days ago I overheard your mother talking to one of her friends. She mentioned you had already doubled the bookings. I think she's impressed."

"I'm glad. Not that she would ever say anything to me."

"Of course not. My mom is exactly the same. I promise myself I won't be like her when my kids are out on their own, but I'm afraid I will be. How does that happen? How do we turn into our mothers?"

"Not a clue." Carly didn't want to think she was anything like her mother, but she had a feeling they had more in common than she wanted to admit.

"Maybe I'll do better with this one," Maribel said, glancing down at her stomach.

"You did great with the others."

"I did okay. I learned from each of them. After all this time one would think I would be perfect, but I know that's not true."

"Yeah, I make plenty of mistakes." Carly glanced out at the gardens. "Do you think it's the least bit possible that our kids understand we're trying to do our best?"

"Not a prayer."

"You're right. I would never have believed that of my mom." Carly still didn't.

"It is a mother's lot in life to be misunderstood and underappreciated. That's why we get our own day." Maribel pushed herself into standing position and groaned. "I'm going to go home where I can lie down and remember what it was like when I could see my feet."

"Okay. Have a good afternoon."

"You, too."

Carly turned back to her computer and opened the spreadsheet. She wanted to finish this projection, then start calling some of the local bridal fairs. If it wasn't too late, she would buy a booth and plan on selling the B and B as a great place to hold a wedding. But before she could finish entering the information into her program, the phone rang.

"Chatsworth-by-the-Sea," Carly said. "May I help you?"

"I would like to speak with Carly Spencer please."

"That's me."

"Mrs. Spencer, this is Mrs. Beecham, the vice principal. I have Tiffany in my office."

"What?" Carly's stomach flopped over and dove for her toes. No. This wasn't happening.

"I'm sorry to inform you that your daughter has been cutting class. Is it possible for you to come to the school anytime soon?"

Carly had already logged out of her program. "I'll be right there."

It had only been three weeks, Carly thought grimly as she parked on the street, then hurried in the main entrance. Three weeks. Tiffany had never once gotten in this kind of trouble at her old school.

Worse, Carly had thought things had been improving with her daughter. Tiffany had made a couple of friends, including a girl who had stayed for dinner a couple of nights ago. There was even a boy she liked—Jack something. She mentioned meeting him in the computer lab and how she hoped he liked her. So why this?

Carly followed the familiar halls to the vice principal's office and went inside. Tiffany sat on a bench outside a closed door. She rose when she saw her mother.

"You didn't bring Grandma," she said, sounding both scared and relieved.

"No. I didn't tell her." Carly hadn't wanted to hear the lecture. "I'll explain things to her after I understand them myself."

Tiffany grabbed her arm. "It's not what you think. It's not bad. I didn't do anything wrong. Well, not bad-wrong. Mom, I can explain. It's not my fault."

"How many times have I heard that sentence before?"

"But it's true."

The door opened and Mrs. Beecham stepped out.

The woman was in her early thirties, attractive and well dressed. Not exactly the dried-up old prune Carly remembered from *her* days at the school. Apparently administrators had changed in the past twenty-two years. But the rules hadn't, and if Tiffany was cutting class, there was going to be hell to pay both here and at home.

"Mrs. Spencer?" the vice principal asked with a smile.

"It's very nice to meet you, although I'm sorry it has to be under these circumstances."

"Me, too," Carly said as they shook hands.

Tiffany tightened her grip on her arm. "Mom, I'm really, really telling the truth. I didn't do anything wrong."

"Why don't you let us discuss it?" Mrs. Beecham said pleasantly. "Would you prefer your daughter in with us or would you like to have her wait out here?"

Tiffany's blue eyes pleaded for admission to the meeting. Carly hesitated. The situation was a new one. She still couldn't believe this was happening. Tiffany had acted up before, but she'd never done it at school. Skipping classes? Was it possible.

"She can join us," she said, not sure if she was making the right decision.

"Thanks." Tiffany moved close. "I can explain everything."

Mrs. Beecham frowned. "You'll have to be quiet if you're to sit with us," she said sternly. "Do I make myself clear?"

Tiffany shivered slightly and nodded.

Carly followed the vice principal into her bright and cheerful office and took one of the two chairs on the visitor side of the desk. Several plaques hung on the wall, honoring the school for academic achievement. There were mentions of the various universities Mrs. Beecham had attended and Carly was a little surprised to see her first name was Heather. Somehow women named Heather had never been so authoritarian before. At least not in her world.

"Tiffany has missed her class after lunch twice this week," Mrs. Beecham said. "I can see by her transcripts that she was never in this sort of trouble before, which is why I wanted to have you in, Mrs. Spencer. We don't want to start a negative pattern here in Tiffany's new school."

"I don't get it," Carly said, turning to her daughter. "You're cutting class after lunch? What's going on? Are you leaving campus?"

"That's not permitted until one is a senior," Mrs. Beecham said quietly.

Tiffany ignored her. "I'm not going anywhere. I've been working in the computer lab. On stuff for the B and B. That's what I've been trying to tell you. I was working on the computer doing graphic designs. I lost track of time and didn't realize I should be in class. I messed up and I was late. But here, if you're more than ten minutes late, it counts as an unexcused absence. Which means they're saying I cut class, but I was really there."

Carly turned to Mrs. Beecham. "Is that true? Is more than a ten-minute tardy an unexcused absence?"

The other woman nodded. "It may seem harsh, but we

want to make sure the students are in class, learning. People strolling in ten or fifteen minutes after the bell disrupts the class for everyone."

Carly saw her point—sort of. But if a kid was late to class, it seemed wrong to tag her with cutting school.

"I'll make sure Tiffany understands it's important to be in class on time," Carly said. "What is her punishment?"

"Two days of detention."

Tiffany gasped. Before she could say anything, Carly shot her a warning look.

"All right. Thanks, Mrs. Beecham. I assume you have some system in place so that Tiffany can get back to class without being marked down for truancy?"

"Of course. I'll write her a pass."

"Great. If I could have a minute to speak with her in the hall, I'd really appreciate it."

"Of course."

"But I—"

Tiffany started to speak. Carly grabbed her hand and pulled her to her feet.

"We'll be right outside," she said. "I'll send her in to get the note."

"Good. Thank you so much for coming right away. I feel it's very important to nip this sort of thing in the bud."

"Of course. Sure. Have a nice day."

Carly led Tiffany into the hallway and closed the door behind them.

"It's not fair," Tiffany wailed. "I can't believe this is happening because I was late."

Carly found herself wanting to agree, yet unwilling to side with her daughter against the vice principal.

"I don't necessarily agree with the rules, but it's good to know what they are so you can avoid getting into trouble the next time."

"But I was doing stuff for *you*."

Carly put an arm around her. "I know, and I really appreciate it. But I'm thinking maybe it's time to spend your lunch hour doing something else. Trust me—you don't want a career of detention."

"I can't believe she's making me do that. I'm not some loser."

"Agreed, but it could be worse. It could be three days."

Her daughter grimaced. "I wasn't doing it on purpose. You know that, right?"

"I do. I've seen how engrossed you get in your work. I believe that you didn't hear the bell."

Tiffany looked relieved. "Thanks, Mom. This was all so

horrible. She called me out of class and everything. Talk about total humiliation. I thought I'd just die."

Just then a tall, skinny guy with short brown hair and shoulders broad enough to support the world rounded the corner. He jogged toward them.

"Tiff. Jeez, I'm really sorry." He noticed Carly and skidded to a stop. "Oh, hi. Are you Tiffany's mom?"

"Yes. Carly Spencer."

"Hey. I'm Jack. I've been hanging out with Tiffany in the computer lab. This is totally my fault. I have the computer lab right after lunch so I've learned to tune out the bells. I should have been paying attention and made sure she got back to class on time."

So this was Jack—the boy Tiffany had been talking about. He was charming, in a puppy-dog kind of way. Carly liked how he took responsibility—something her daughter could learn to do.

"I've been helping her with the graphic designs," he continued. "She's really talented."

Tiffany stared at the floor and blushed. "No, you are," she mumbled. "Jack's come up with some great ideas for colors."

He shrugged. "I'm really interested in the house, Mrs. Spencer. I've heard about it for years, but I've never been. The ghost thing. Totally cool. I've been doing some research on ghosts and paranormal phenomenon. I've even bought some equipment, you know, to help find it."

Tiffany looked at him. "My mom's seen the ghost."

"For real?"

"Not recently," Carly said. "That was years ago. You should come out and look around."

His face brightened. He glanced at Tiffany and seemed to almost glow. "Thank you for asking. I'd like that very much. Look, um, I have to get back to class. I just wanted to let you know that it wasn't Tiffany's fault."

He smiled at her, winked at her daughter, then loped away.

Carly watched him go. Okay, he was a good kid with decent manners. She liked that and she liked him. Of course saying that was a really bad idea.

"He's older, isn't he?" she asked instead.

"Just by a year. He's sixteen." Tiffany sighed. "He has his license. Do you think he likes me?"

"I don't know. Maybe. I'm not sure about him, though."

Tiffany rolled her eyes. "You don't like anyone I like. So why did you invite him over?"

"So I can keep an eye on him and you."

"I hate my life."

"I'm sure you do. Look, go get your note from Mrs.

Beecham and head to class. I'll be by after your detention to pick you up."

Tiffany nodded, but before she turned away, she asked, "What's my punishment at home?"

Carly almost asked "For what?" when she remembered the tardiness. She weighed the options and decided to go with her gut.

"You've never done this before," she said. "I think there are extenuating circumstances. Your detention is enough."

Tiffany's whole face brightened. "Yeah?"

"Yeah."

Her daughter flung her arms around her and hugged her hard. "You're the best, Mom."

"I am pretty cool, aren't I?"

Carly had barely taken two steps when she saw Mr. Everwood, aka Steve, approaching.

"We meet again," he said, looking handsome in a math-teacher sort of way. "I heard about Tiffany. I think the tardy rule takes things a little too far, but I don't make the rules."

"Me, either. But it's handled."

"How are you settling in?"

"Getting there. I'm working hard at the B and B. It's fun, but challenging."

"I heard there were some changes."

"That's true."

"I'd love to hear the details. How about over dinner?"

The man was too smooth by far, Carly thought.

"I, uh, dinner." With Mr. Everwood? Could she really do that? "Um, sure. Great."

"I'll give you a call."

She nodded and started backing toward the main entrance. "I know you know the number. Thanks. I, uh, I have to get back to work. Good to see you."

"You, too, Carly."

She turned to bolt, but before she could get up any speed, he called her back.

"How are we doing on the whole 'calling me by my first name' thing?" he asked with a grin.

"It's much better."

"You're lying."

"Okay. I'm working on it."

"Keep practicing."

Carly watched her mother debate which side to come down on. Tiffany shouldn't be late to class, but this was her beloved granddaughter and she had been working to help the B and B.

"You've spoken with her?" Rhonda asked.

"Yes, and she has detention for two days. That should be unpleasant enough to remind her to get back in class on time."

"Are you punishing her?"

Carly debated how to handle the situation. Right now she couldn't face another run-in with her mother on how to raise Tiffany.

"I was going to," she said carefully. "But then I remembered what you always said—that the punishment should fit the crime. As Tiffany wasn't trying to skip class and get away with anything, I think the detention is enough."

Rhonda considered the answer, then nodded. "I agree. She's basically a sweet girl. With a little more direction and parenting, she'll grow up into a fine young woman."

Carly clenched her teeth, then did her best to relax. Remember the bigger picture, she told herself. Better to keep things pleasant in the family, at least during all the changes in the B and B.

Besides, she knew one sure way to make her mother forget all about Tiffany.

"I ran into Steve Everwood while I was at the high school," she said as she poured them each a glass of lemonade. "I think he's going to call and ask me out to dinner."

Rhonda's shock was priceless. Carly wasn't sure if her

mother was surprised that a man would be interested or that Carly would talk about it.

"Well, good for you," Rhonda said as she took a glass. "He's supposed to be very nice. He has a steady job and everyone says he was good to his late wife. You knew he was a widower, didn't you? He's not divorced. I've heard he does what he can to get women in bed and then he dumps them, but I doubt you'll have a problem with that."

There was so much information in her mother's short speech, Carly didn't know what to respond to first. Was her mother implying she wouldn't have a problem with Steve's amorous nature because he wasn't likely to be interested in her that way, or because she was such a slut that she could easily handle it? And what was up with making a point of him being a widower rather than divorced?

Well, at least she had the distraction she'd wanted.

"I'm not sure if I want to go out with him," Carly said. "He was my teacher in high school. That makes the whole thing kind of weird."

"That was nearly twenty-five years ago. What does it matter now?"

Technically not yet twenty-two years, Carly thought.

"Besides, you'll be forty soon," her mother added. "You'd better accept any invitations that come your way."

"Before I'm too old," Carly said, not sure if she should laugh or scream.

"Exactly. You could do worse than him."

"Good to know." How thrilling that she had yet to hit bottom.

CHAPTER 7

"This is all your fault," Rhonda complained loudly.

At least that's what Carly *thought* she was saying. She'd never been very good at reading lips and it was impossible to hear actual words over the whine of twenty or thirty remote-control model airplanes swooping and soaring off the cliffs.

The sound was incredible—part chainsaw, part lawnmower, but at a pitch designed to send onlookers into madness.

She motioned for her mother to follow her back into the B and B where they could speak in relatively normal tones.

"What was that?" she asked when she'd closed the door behind them.

Her mother glared at her. "I blame you for that. The noise is horrible. How long are they here for?"

"Three nights." Carly did her best not to look too happy,

but in truth, she was giddy with delight. "Three whole nights with the B and B full and local restaurants catering the meals. We get a cut of that, you know. A smooth fifteen percent off the top."

"I don't like it. I already have a headache."

Carly did, too, but she figured it was a small price to pay for wild success.

Okay, maybe not *wild success*, but a really big step in the right direction.

"We're lucky to have them," she said. "Their usual hotel had a lot of damage after last winter's storms so they were looking for a place. We have everything they want, including the cliffs where they can fly their planes. They're just one chapter of a fairly large national organization. We could have clubs like this here all the time."

Her mother stared at her. "You say that like it's a good thing."

"It is. Just think of the money. Plus, I've been able to put together some special activities on a small scale. We have that lecturer coming in tonight to talk about the history of the house. That should be fun. If he's any good, I'll book him regularly."

Maribel had turned her on to a professor at the community college who had done a lot of research on Chatsworth-by-the-Sea and was considered the resident expert on the ghost.

Carly was looking forward to attending the lecture herself and maybe learning something. Like where Mary had been hiding out all these weeks.

She walked into the main office and pointed to the booking schedule posted on the far wall.

"We're booking up faster than I thought we would. Those ghost hunters are here next weekend. We still have the horror writers coming and there's a group that researches paranormal phenomenon coming at the end of the month. I've already received calls from three former guests who are interested in reserving rooms. They said the drive was longer than they liked for a weekend, but it was worth it for a chance to hang with a ghost."

Her mother studied the chart. "We're starting to fill up."

"I know. It's fabulous. If things keep going like this, we might break even for the month of August."

"So soon?"

"Don't get too excited. It's just one month, but we're moving in the right direction. I want to do some more brainstorming. I was thinking of a Regency-themed weekend. We could hold cooking classes and learn the dances from the time."

"You're certainly pushing our ghost."

"She's the best selling point we have. Without her, I couldn't make this work."

Her mother shook her head. "People are so silly about ghosts."

"As long as those people are interested in booking rooms, I don't care how silly they are."

It had only been five weeks, and already Carly could see her work coming to fruition. Talk about a great feeling. There hadn't been any more calls from the school about Tiffany, which was a good thing. Neil had actually called his daughter three times. Life was good. Now if she could grow the business steadily, she would be a happy camper.

"Has Steve called?" Rhonda asked.

Carly's good mood took a decided turn for the unsettled.

"Um, yeah. Last week. He asked me to dinner but we had that group in and I had to stay and supervise the evening."

"You turned down a date with him to stay home and work?"

The tone of her mother's voice implied she was not only stupid, but she might have lost the only opportunity she would ever have to date again.

"The B and B has to get all my attention right now."

"You can take an evening off when a nice man asks you

out to dinner. You're never going to get married again if you don't put yourself out there."

Had Carly been drinking, she would have choked. "What? Married? Why would I want to do that?"

"Do you want to spend the rest of your life alone?"

"Frankly, that doesn't sound so bad. Mom, I was married for over sixteen years. I'm kind of enjoying being on my own."

"What woman *wants* to be alone?"

"A lot of them." Married. Yuck. "I'm still recovering from my time with Neil."

"The best way to get over a bad fall is to get right back on the horse. I would have myself except no one could measure up to your father."

"I'm through riding." Although Maribel's comment about sex popped into her head. It had been a really long time. She might not want to commit to any one man, but some time in bed had a certain appeal.

Of course having sex with a man meant getting naked. The last time she'd done that with someone new, she'd been twenty and pretty damned hot. While she wasn't hideous now, she was a couple of days shy of forty and she'd had a child. No one would look at her body and use the word *perky* to describe anything. There were stretch marks and squishy bits and some odd bulges she couldn't get rid of.

Obviously the solution was to find a way to have sex with her clothes on. Or in very, very subtle lighting. Or with someone so incredibly desperate that he would only feel amazing gratitude that she was willing to be with him at all.

Carly's reluctance to date Steve came back to bite her in the butt less than five hours later. And it started so innocently, too.

"Jack asked me out," Tiffany said that night over dinner.

The clear evening was blessedly silent, what with all the model plane folks busy eating their catered dinner in the main dining room.

"That's nice," Carly told her. "You know the rule."

"But it's not fair. I can't help it if I'm not sixteen yet. If you'd had me earlier, I could be sixteen now and go out with him."

"Yes. And although I did specifically plan my pregnancy so that fifteen years later I could ruin your life, the answer stays the same. No dating until you're sixteen."

"Just because you're not interested in men, Carly, is no reason to infringe on your daughter's happiness," Rhonda said as she passed the salad.

"Yeah," Tiffany said smugly.

Carly clutched her fork while the shower scene music from *Psycho* played in her head.

"Thanks for the thought, Mom," Carly said, wishing there was wine with dinner. "But Tiffany is too young to be out alone with a guy." She turned to her daughter. "You're more than welcome to have Jack over here where you two can hang out in a very supervised way."

"You mean so you can spy on us."

"Pretty much," Carly admitted cheerfully.

Tiffany rolled her eyes as she turned to her grandmother. "She thinks we're going to have sex. We're not. I know all about it and I'm not interested."

Carly completely believed her. At that age, she'd been far more interested in romance than sex. Right until some slightly older guy had kissed her senseless and then touched her breasts in a way that had made her want to explore the possibilities.

"Tiffany seems very trustworthy," Rhonda said.

"I agree. But my decision stays the same. No dating this year."

"But I *hate* having Jack over," Tiffany complained. "He's so interested in the stupid house and the stupid ghost. He wants to check out all the rooms with some dumb equipment he bought so he can figure out where she is. I swear, he's more interested in that ghost than in me."

Which made Carly really like the boy.

"Plus, he wants you to be with him, so you can tell him where you've seen the ghost," Tiffany added, sounding outraged.

"Your boyfriend isn't interested in your mother," Rhonda said, patting her granddaughter's arm.

"I know. It's just weird."

Carly changed the subject by asking about Tiffany's progress on the new letterhead. From there, they moved into a spirited discussion on the best kind of swimsuit for summer and if they should sell "beach packs" to guests wanting water—a towel and some suntan lotion. The meal ended without anymore mention of Jack, dating, or Carly's inability to attract men.

When her mother and her daughter had disappeared—Rhonda to open the mail and Tiffany to check out the latest fashions on the Style network—Carly retreated to her office where she leaned back in her chair and breathed in the silence.

This was good, she thought, hoping her pleasure in the moment didn't jinx it. She was working hard and it was paying off, big-time. Sure, she still had five billion things to do, but in the meantime, she was happy and making progress.

Then her mother walked into the office and put a letter on her desk.

"We're going to have a new guest," Rhonda said.

"Okay. And this is important, why?"

"Because he's going to try and ruin us. This always happens. Why can't they just leave us alone?"

Carly sat up in her chair and reached for the letter. It was addressed to her from an Adam Covell. He wanted a large room with a view for three weeks, during which time he would be conducting experiments on the house.

"Experiments?"

"Keep reading."

Carly scanned the rest of the letter. "He's coming to debunk the myth? What? He's a ghostbuster?"

"Apparently. They show up from time to time."

This Carly didn't need. "What are we going to do?" she asked, more to herself than her mother. "Are we expected to produce a ghost? I don't have one right now."

There hadn't been any "shimmering essences" since she and Tiffany had returned. As much as Carly wanted to believe her childhood sightings, there wasn't any proof.

"We haven't had one ever," Rhonda told her. "Sometimes I worry about you. You've been talking about the ghost like this for some time and I couldn't figure out why. It's not real. It never has been. This man is here to ruin us and I don't think we can do anything to stop him."

CHAPTER 8

Carly clutched the arms of her chair. "No one is going to ruin us. I won't let him. Besides, there was something once. I remember seeing things, feeling a presence. Maribel felt it, too."

Rhonda sat down and took her hands. "I know you think you did. When you were little we talked about Mary all the time and I think that made her real to you. But anything you saw was just our usual tricks."

"What?" Carly pulled free and stood. "What tricks? I'll admit believing in ghosts is a stretch of the imagination, but I saw her. Or something shimmery. I saw her walk through walls. I heard her voice."

Rhonda sighed. "I'm so sorry. I never meant for this to hurt you. The stories about the house being haunted have existed for as long as the house has been here. I remember hearing them when I was growing up. People were always interested in the fact that the place was haunted and the family has kept that interest going. It's good for business."

Carly felt odd defending the fact the house was haunted when she wasn't a hundred percent convinced. But she wasn't willing to reject the possibility. "But over the years, dozens of people have tried to prove there's no ghost and they've all walked away believers."

"I know. There are things that can be done to make people believe. Our family has been fooling the public forever. But it's not real. It's never been real. What you're remembering is all the stories, Carly. What we talked about. Mary isn't real and the house has never been haunted."

She didn't want to hear any of this, so she excused herself and walked out of the office. As she moved down the hallway, she studied moldings and doorways and antique pictures. What had, just a few minutes before, seemed charmingly eccentric, now just looked old and dusty. She felt the walls beginning to close in on her.

Carly walked to the edge of the property and stood staring out at the sun sinking over the ocean. The waves were orange and red and gold, the sky nearly white. It was breathtakingly beautiful, but all she could think was that she couldn't take one more kick in the teeth.

She'd lived through an unhappy marriage, staying because she thought it was the right thing to do. She'd endured a divorce, the loss of most of her friends, selling her house and furniture, a move here, only to find out the B and B wasn't going to be a haven after all. By God, she would *not* give up her ghost.

As soon as the thought formed, she felt her lips twitch. Then she started to laugh. *Giving up the ghost*. She'd never understood what the expression meant, and still didn't, but it was appropriate. She wasn't giving up on Mary.

Maybe it hadn't been real to anyone else, but it had been real to her. She wouldn't allow some would-be ghostbuster to take that away from her.

She returned to the house and found her mother in her room.

"What do you mean, you faked Mary," Carly asked. "How come I remember stuff?"

Her mother shook her head. "Your father and I used to fight about your belief in the ghost. I wanted to tell you the truth, but he thought it was charming. And he did a lot of things to convince you she was real."

Carly suddenly understood Tiffany's emotional outbursts at the unfairness of her world when the grown-ups around her did their best to destroy her happiness.

"No," she said, trying to stay calm, but feeling panic build. "Daddy would never have lied to me."

"It wasn't a lie, Carly. It was…something to make you feel special. Come with me."

Her mother led her to the tower Carly had always escaped to when she'd been a kid. They climbed the stairs to the dusty room where Carly had curled up to read. But instead of going inside, her mother showed her a small secret compartment in a wall. After pressing a hidden latch, the door swung open, revealing a kind of slide projector. As Carly watched, her mother turned it on.

"Go back into the tower room," Rhonda told her.

Carly hesitated, then did as she asked. Shock swept through her as she realized a shimmering presence stood gracefully in the corner of the room.

"Mary," she breathed as sharp disappointment cut through her. It wasn't real. None of it had been real.

"There are three or four slides," her mother said. "Your father would use different ones at different times. He worried you were too solitary, and having Mary around gave you a friend."

Carly couldn't believe it. She returned to the hallway. "What else did he do?"

Rhonda turned off the projector. "There are dozens of

tricks. We have specially prepared rooms for nonbelievers where we can change the temperature at will. We can mist their room so they feel a chilly presence. There are tables that tilt, walls that rotate. I'll show you everything before this Adam Covell arrives. I'm sure we can convince him just like we've convinced the others."

"Okay. Yeah. We should probably talk about it," Carly said, still surprised by all the trickery. "Thanks for showing me this."

"Are you all right?" her mother asked.

"Fine." Not really, but what was she going to say? "I'm going back to my office. See you in the morning."

She left her mother in the tower and made her way downstairs.

Intellectually she understood the pain of learning that Mary wasn't real came from a whole lot more than just the loss of a memory. It was the final straw in what had been an emotionally difficult year.

But it didn't feel that way. Disappointment threatened to crush her.

She'd been walking around wondering when Mary was going to show up. She'd called out to her several times and had even started investigating ways to get a ghost to appear. All of which made her feel stupid. She'd been so sure. She'd depended on the reality of having a ghost. She'd—

Carly walked from her office to the side door, then made her way back to the cliffs. Once there, she turned back. The massive old house rose four stories into the evening sky. Huge and beautiful and very, very expensive to keep going.

Disappointment flared into anger. Without the ghost, she didn't have a viable business. She'd been selling Chatsworth-by-the-Sea as a haunted B and B. No one was all that interested in a slightly rundown, very old, former English manor. Without Mary, they were sunk.

Carly might have come here because she didn't have any other choice, but now she was committed. She liked the house and she liked the idea of returning to her roots. After nearly six weeks of hard work, she'd seen plenty of progress. No way was she going to uproot Tiffany and start over in some other place all because of a hotshot guy who thought he was Bill Murray in *Ghostbusters*.

"There is no way in hell you're taking this away from me, Adam Covell."

Carly found her mother in her private sitting room. Tiffany sat next to her on the small chintz-covered sofa. Her daughter's forlorn expression told Carly that she'd been given the news.

"You said we've been fooling other ghostbusters for years," Carly said.

"Oh, there are dozens of ways. There's an old journal full of ideas. I can't remember more than what I told you. Give me a second."

She rose and walked into her bedroom. A few minutes later, she appeared with an old wooden box. "It's all in here."

Carly took the box. "I'm going to find out all I can about our guest and figure out what we can do to defeat him. The success of the B and B depends on us being haunted."

Tiffany's eyes widened. "You're going to lie about Mary?"

"If I have to. It's a matter of survival, and apparently there's a long tradition of it in this family." She clutched the box tightly to her chest. "Tomorrow, as soon as you get home from school, we'll have a family meeting and figure out a plan. Between now and then, I'll go over what's in here and check out this Adam guy on the Internet. Fair enough?"

Tiffany and her grandmother nodded. "We'll be there," Rhonda said. "We'll be ready to kick some ass."

Jack joined their meeting the following afternoon. Carly wasn't sure about discussing such a sensitive issue in front of him, but he insisted on being a part of things.

"I can help," he told her. "I know technology. Maybe I can come up with some ideas or figure out ways to make them work. Please?"

He looked so serious and sincere, she thought wistfully. But what really sold her was Tiffany's pleading expression. After all, fooling Adam would allow her to spend time with Jack, which wasn't exactly as good as dating, but pretty close.

Carly set her papers down on the coffee table in front of the sofa in the rear parlor they'd temporarily taken over.

"Technical help would be nice," she said. "As you all know, we get most of our business because we're haunted. We're featured on the national ghost registry as a haunting that has never been disproved. It's like getting a five-star safety rating. But if one of the top ghostbusters disproves the haunting, we're removed from the registry and marked as a hoax. Not good for our bottom line."

"No kidding," Jack said.

"What are we going to do?" Tiffany asked.

"Fight back. I spent a lot of time on the Internet, and Adam Covell is going to be difficult to defeat. Apparently he comes from a long line of people interested in debunking rumors about paranormal phenomenon. His grandfather made a living doing it and wrote a lot of books." She held up the one she'd checked out of the library that morning.

"I couldn't find out very much on Adam himself," she continued. "He doesn't do this with the same enthusiasm as his grandfather, but he's just as deadly. He wrote papers on two supposedly haunted houses in Virginia. One was a restaurant and the other an inn. Both closed within a year of his report."

Rhonda caught her breath. "A year? We can't let that happen. Carly, did you go over those papers I gave you?"

"Every one of them." She set the box on the table. "We're going to assign Adam to the special bedroom. It's been fitted with two secret entrances, a misting system and its own heating and cooling units."

"Why?" Tiffany asked. "What will that do?"

"The heating and cooling will allow for fast temperature changes," Jack said eagerly. "Misting him will give him a chill. And you can use the secret entrances to take stuff in and out of his room." He looked at Carly. "Is that right?"

"Yes. It's exactly right. We want to keep Mr. Covell on his toes."

"Can we poison him?" Rhonda asked.

Carly stared at her mother. "What are you talking about? We want him impressed, not dead."

"Oh, I didn't mean kill him. But if he had an upset stomach the whole time he was here, he couldn't do his best work."

Fooling a man was one thing, but compromising his health was another. "No poison," Carly said firmly. "Our goal is make sure our guest believes he's been thoroughly haunted. Then he'll go away and we can get on with our lives."

They talked for another half hour. Carly passed out assignments, including several for herself. She wanted to make sure the special equipment was in working order.

When she was alone in the parlor, she drew in a deep breath. As much as she knew she had to convince Adam there was a ghost, a part of her simply wanted to give up and cry. How could she have lost such an important part of her past so easily?

She supposed that in the scheme of things, believing in a ghost in the first place was a little stupid. No one else did. But Mary had been a part of her memories for a long time. She'd accepted her because, to Carly, she'd existed.

And now she'd not only lost someone she'd thought of as a friend, but she might be losing the B and B.

"Not gonna happen," she told herself. They had a plan. More important, they had desperation on their side. She was reminded of the old story about a rabbit being chased by a hound. When the rabbit got away, the hound was teased for being too slow. He'd pointed out that while he'd been running for his supper, the rabbit had been running for its life. She and her family were the rabbit and there was no way in hell that hound was going to catch them.

"Do you like it?" Tiffany asked anxiously.

Carly picked through the cheerful basket of office supplies her daughter had bought for her. "I love everything," she said with a laugh. "You know I can't resist things like folders and paper clips."

They sat at a table, outside, facing the ocean. The afternoon was warm, the sky a blue only found on the California coast. After a late lunch of all of Carly's favorites, they'd moved on to celebrating her fortieth birthday with presents and a large cake.

Carly fingered the gold bracelet her mother had bought her. The delicate links made her feel feminine—a nice change from her constant attempts to be businesslike and in charge. She'd been concerned that finding herself almost divorced, alone and forty would be too depressing for words, but so far she was doing fine.

A testament to the human spirit, she thought as a large black SUV pulled into the parking lot.

She glanced over as the door opened and a man stepped out. He was tall, with too-long dark hair and a lean, hard body designed to make women look twice.

Her gaze swept over his flat stomach and broad shoulders before settling on a face that was both chiseled and incredibly handsome. His large, dark eyes defined soulful, while his mouth made her think about kissing in ways she hadn't in maybe twenty years.

Gorgeous, she thought, breathlessly. Young…too young, but gorgeous.

He saw them and waved, then strolled over. Carly liked the way he walked—all purposeful stride and narrow hips.

"Afternoon," he said in a low voice that made her want to sigh. "I'm Adam Covell and I'm looking for Carly Spencer. I have a reservation."

"I'm Carly," she said. "Welcome to Chatsworth-by-the-Sea."

She rose and held out her hand. When he shook it she felt definite sparkage, as her daughter would say.

Adam looked her over and grinned. "Nice to meet you."

Oh, yeah, she thought cheerfully. Happy birthday to me.

CHAPTER 9

"**If** you'd just sign the registration card," Carly said after she'd led Adam into the house and to the main desk.

He glanced over the preprinted lines, then signed his name with a bold, black slash of letters.

"Don't you want to yell at me?" he asked. "Most owners do. They take me to task and call me names."

"I had that planned for the second half of our evening," Carly told him, still caught up in his appearance. She couldn't remember the last time a guy had gotten her attention on such a physical level. Was it her? Had the divorce freed her to look in a way she never would have let herself before? Or was it more than that? Was Adam simply one of those guys who captured a woman's interest and didn't let go?

He topped her by about six or seven inches. Even casually dressed—in jeans and a tucked-in T-shirt—he exuded confidence and power.

Yum, yum, she thought, even as she knew she was flirting with a danger she would never embrace. He couldn't be much more than thirty. Should she ever get the courage to do the naked thing, it was going to be with a guy a whole lot more desperate than this one. She doubted Adam had ever spent even one evening unwillingly alone.

"I will admit that if you're trying to ruin us, it seems tacky to actually stay here," she admitted as she handed him a key, then led the way to the elevator.

"I do it for two reasons," he told her. "First, I need to be close by to figure out how you're faking out your guests. Those kinds of tricks require a lot of personal observation. The second reason is to contribute to the business cash flow. It's the least I can do."

"Gee, so you want to help before you try to put us out of business. How generous. *And* you're calling me a liar. What a popular guest you must be everywhere you go."

"'Liar' is harsh."

"But it's what you mean."

She pushed the up button and turned to face him. His dark eyes seemed to stare into her soul. She wanted to swoon right there on the hardwood floor and hope that he would catch her.

"I grew up here," she said, instead of collapsing. "I have memories of time spent with our ghost. She used to come in my bedroom and read with me. We walked in the garden. We were friends."

A slight exaggeration, she thought, as she smiled brightly.

"You really believe in your ghost," he said, sounding faintly surprised.

"As much as I believe in you."

The elevator doors opened and she stepped inside.

Adam followed her and set his small suitcase on the floor.

"Not much luggage for a three-week stay."

"The rest of it is in my rental. I have a lot of equipment I'll be setting up."

Oh, joy. A techno-ghostbuster. Just her luck.

"Have you ever found a ghost?" she asked.

"No. They don't exist. Not even your Mary."

"You know her name?"

"I know everything about her. Mary Cunningham. The second daughter to a baron. She married at eighteen, moved to this house, never had children and died at twenty-two. From all accounts, her death was caused by food poisoning."

They reached the third floor. Carly stepped into the hallway.

"I never knew how she died," she admitted.

She paused in front of his door and held out her hand for the key. When he handed it to her, their fingers brushed. She felt more sparkage. It was like being sixteen again. Maybe hanging around Adam would help her relate to her daughter better, she thought with a grin.

"This is one of our larger rooms," she said as she pushed open the door and entered. "You're on the corner, so you have a perfect view of the ocean and the cliffs to our north."

She walked around the big, open space, showing him the armoire, the television and remote, the entrance to the small bathroom.

"Breakfast is served from seven until nine-thirty during the week and until eleven on weekends. We'll provide a box lunch with a day's notice. There's a menu in your desk. As for dinner, we don't have a restaurant, but you can either drive into town or call one of the restaurants and have something delivered. That list is in your desk, as well."

"You have it all covered," he said with an easy grin. "Nice place."

Sure. Right before he destroyed it. "Why us?" she asked. "Why don't you go debunk some other place and leave us alone?"

"You have the most highly documented haunted house

in the area. I've wanted to come here for a long time, but I knew I would need at least three weeks. I had to wait until my schedule permitted."

"Lucky us."

He crossed to the window and stared out. "Is she your daughter?"

Carly joined him and glanced down at the lawn. Tiffany sat with her grandmother. Jack had joined them.

"Yes."

"She's pretty. She must get that from you."

The compliment made her laugh. "Very smooth. Get to me through my daughter. I'll give you points for being good, but don't expect to win me over."

He turned to her. "You can't blame me for trying. But now that I've shown my hand, you'll probably want to keep a close eye on me."

She opened her mouth, then closed it. Was he *flirting* with her? On purpose?

"You'd better stay on the straight and narrow," she said. "Or I'll send my mother after you. Trust me, you don't want that."

"You're right." Adam leaned against the window frame and crossed his arms over his chest. "You have beautiful eyes."

She resisted the sudden need to flutter her eyelashes at him. This guy was good—and way too experienced for her.

"I'll bet you say that to all the girls."

"Only when it's true."

She felt definite heat low in her belly—the first flickering interests of sexual desire.

That can't be smart, she thought. Adam was too good-looking and way out of her league. It was probably best to make a speedy retreat.

"I hope you enjoy your stay here," she said, backing out of the room. "Call down to the desk if you have any questions."

"Will do."

She nodded and left. It was only after she was in the hall that she remembered he was trying to discredit her and that she shouldn't make friends with the enemy. If he was going to spend the next three weeks proving the ghost didn't exist, Carly was going to spend just as long trying to show him she did. There was no way she could be attracted to him.

Except she was, and damn if it didn't feel really good.

"So?" her mother asked as Carly approached the picnic table. "What did he say?"

"Hi, Jack," Carly said as she took her seat. "He was very

polite, very nice and very insistent that we didn't have a ghost. Apparently he has a bunch of equipment in his SUV. I have a feeling he's a technical kind of guy."

"We can beat him," Jack said with the confidence of a sixteen-year-old who has yet to experience serious defeat. "He's toast."

"Hope so."

"He's very handsome," Rhonda said. "Those dark eyes. Was he charming? He seemed charming."

"He was okay," Carly said as she picked at a roll. No way was she going to discuss her suddenly squishy insides with her mother or her daughter.

"You're right, Grandma," Tiffany said dreamily as she stared at the house. "I mean he's really old and everything, but he was hot."

Jack narrowed his gaze. "You liked him?" he asked in outrage.

Tiffany seemed to surface. She glanced at Jack and smiled. "Not like that. He's practically old enough to be my dad." Then she glanced at Carly and her smile widened.

Carly shook her head. Great. Adam Covell had been in residence all of fifteen minutes and he already had the three generations of women lusting after him. What would happen over the next couple of weeks?

"Maybe you can go out with him," her daughter said.

Before Carly could answer, Rhonda chimed in. "Nonsense. She's already dating Steve Everwood."

Tiffany's mouth dropped open. "You're dating my math teacher? Mo-om. No. You can't. That's just too twisted for words."

Tell me about it, Carly thought. "I'm not dating anyone. In case neither of you has noticed, there aren't any guys around here. So no one has to panic."

"But you will be dating Steve," Rhonda said in a way that made it sound a lot more like a statement than a question.

"I'm not so sure." Carly still had trouble thinking of the man as "Steve." She had a feeling it would be better to hold off on any dating until she could work her mind around his first name. Plus, "I'm really busy with work. I don't have time."

"You need to make time," Rhonda told her.

Not likely. "Until that happens, let's focus on what's important. We have to make sure we stay one step ahead of our new guest. By the time he leaves here, I want him totally convinced we have a haunted house with a beautiful and active ghost in residence."

Early the next morning Carly headed out to the garden to pick herbs for Maribel. In her friend's present condition, asking her to bend over was just plain cruel. Besides, Carly enjoyed the quiet of the early hours, before guests were awake and the predawn mist had cleared away.

She collected a basket from the mudroom and stepped out into the cool morning. The sun had yet to clear the mountains behind the B and B, but the sky was bright blue and birds took flight overhead.

She rounded the corner toward the herb garden when the sight of a man by the toolshed stopped her in her tracks. Someone was up very early.

"Morning," Adam called when he saw her.

"Good morning. What on earth are you doing?"

He had just pushed a tall metal pole into the ground. On top was a small platform. He attached a blinking device to it, tightening screws to hold it in place.

"Setting up sensors," he said. "Don't worry. I'll sign whatever you want, saying you're not responsible for my equipment. If it gets hit or knocked over, I won't sue."

She eyed the odd, blinking gray box with the dozens of switches. "What if it gets stolen?"

He grinned. "It has a tracking device, so it's easy to find the thief."

Too bad. Of course if she casually tossed it into the ocean, he wouldn't know it was her. But she wouldn't—for two reasons. First, it was wrong. Second, she hated to pollute the water, and Lord knew what kind of toxic metals were in that thing.

He finished his work and wiped his hands on his jeans, which drew her attention to his butt. Nice, she thought with more than a little appreciation.

He looked good—a long-sleeved shirt rolled up to the elbows, the worn jeans that hugged all the interesting places. Funny how she'd never been one to pay attention to a man's appearance before. Neil was okay-looking. Sure, when they'd first met she'd thought he was cute, but that hadn't been on her list of requirements. Yet with Adam, she had trouble getting past the handsome face and great body to the man inside, so to speak. In fact, she wasn't sure she was interested in the man inside. Which meant there was something seriously wrong with her.

"So what do your sensors do?" she asked as she crouched down in the herb garden and snipped off some basil.

"I'm measuring changes in energy. Are there sudden electromagnetic bursts? Is there an energy field that can't be explained away by an engine or wave generator?"

"You can tell that sort of thing from that little box?"

"Sure. I've set up four more just like it all around the property."

"For someone who doesn't believe in ghosts, you have some fairly serious equipment."

"This is nothing. You should see what I have in my room."

Carly snipped off a few more basil leaves. Had that been an invitation? Did she want it to be?

"How did you come to be in this profession?"

He chuckled. "You mean why am I a ghostbuster?"

She sat back on her heels and looked at him. "Yeah. It's not something they discuss in those guidance sessions in high school."

"I learned from my grandfather. He was really into the whole paranormal thing. When I was a kid, he would take me out with him to various houses."

"Randolph Covell," she said, remembering her Internet research. "He was fairly famous in the field."

"You know about him?"

"I've heard a few things. So you've been dabbling in this all your life and you've never once found a ghost?"

"Not even a near-miss. They don't exist."

So she'd recently heard. Carly supposed it was easier to believe there weren't ghosts than there were, but she still hated the idea of giving up her memories of Mary.

She moved on to the rosemary and cut off a few stalks. "If this is just a hobby, what do you do in your regular life?"

"I develop solid fuels for boosters that send satellites into space."

She tilted her head. "Which means what?"

"I'm a rocket scientist."

Of course he was, she thought glumly. Couldn't they have gotten a ghostbuster existing on the dull-normal side of the IQ chart? But no. They had to get a rocket scientist.

"Tell me there isn't any solid fuel sitting in your bedroom," she said. "We're interested in staying right where we are."

"Not to worry. Although I do have a great thermal imaging system."

"What's that?"

"It takes pictures of my room at regular intervals, but instead of using regular film, it measures changes in temperature. So if something cold or hot passes through, I'll have a record. The room is set at sixty-eight degrees. Your body temperature should be about ninety-eight. So if you went into my room and moved the furniture around, you'd show up on the thermal imaging, even in the dark."

Interesting. That meant they would have to modify their plan. "I would never do that," she said primly as she cut a little more rosemary, then stood and collected her basket. "Mary is going to do all the work of convincing you."

"I hope so. I would like to be wrong once."

"Somehow I doubt that. Have you ever been wrong?"

His dark gaze seemed to linger on her face. "Dozens of times."

She felt a definite pull, as if he was willing her to step into his embrace where he could grab her and kiss her senseless. But as she was reasonably confident the only thing senseless was her, she restrained herself.

"It's about time for breakfast," she said brightly. "Let me take you inside and show you the dining room."

She led the way into the house. "Just through there," she said as she paused in the doorway.

None of the other guests was down yet. Her mother and Tiffany were already seated at a table in the corner. When Rhonda saw Adam, she waved him over.

"Mr. Covell, do join us. You're up early this beautiful morning."

"Mrs. Washington. A pleasure."

Her mother beamed. "Oh, you can call me Rhonda. And you met Tiffany yesterday, didn't you?"

"Yes. Of course. Hi."

"You can sit here," Tiffany said, pulling out the chair next to her.

Her grandmother beat her to it by standing and ushering Adam to the seat beside her. "You'll have a better view from here, Adam."

Carly sighed and turned away. The man was nothing but trouble.

Back in the kitchen she found Maribel slipping a quiche into the oven. Fresh muffins and scones sat cooling on a rack.

"I heard there's a new guy," her friend said as she straightened.

"Oh, yeah. He's here to prove our ghost isn't real and create trouble all at the same time. Even as we speak, my mother and my daughter are fighting for his attention."

"That good-looking, huh?"

"You bet. And charming. And here to destroy us. So I'm going to do my best not to get friendly."

Maribel leaned against the counter. "But you're tempted?"

Carly grinned. "More than a little. There's something really appealing about him. But he's too young and I'm not in the market."

"How young?"

"Early thirties."

"You've just turned forty. That's doable. Guys do it all the time."

"Oh, and you're saying that makes it right?"

"Sure." Maribel waggled her eyebrows. "Think of it as standing up for women everywhere. Being strong. Giving men a taste of their own medicine."

"Thanks, but I don't think so. Besides, I don't even know what I'd do with the guy. Date him? I haven't been on a date in nearly twenty years. I wouldn't know what to do. And if we're talking about sex, forget it. He's far too pretty. I'm sure his last bed partner was twenty-two and perfect."

"Guys have a thing about older women. They believe we can teach them the secrets of being a good lover."

"In this case, he's sadly mistaken."

"You should think about it."

Carly shook her head. "I don't have time. Besides, I'm guessing all the attraction is one-sided. Adam would no more consider dating me than he would ask out my mother."

"I think you're wrong."

"I really appreciate the support. You're a sweetie for saying all this."

"Well, one of us has to be having a thrilling life," Maribel said as she straightened and headed to the counter. "I'm just getting bigger by the second."

"But soon you'll have a baby."

Her friend's expression softened. "I know. Isn't it a miracle?"

"Absolutely."

Carly could think of a lot of words to describe getting pregnant the year she turned forty, and *miracle* wasn't one of them. As she had thought the first time she realized her friend was "with child"—no way, no how. She was happy to have Tiffany, but she wasn't interested in starting over with a newborn.

Not that it was an issue. Even if there was an interested guy, who was to say her eggs were still functioning? No doubt they'd long since turned to raisins and were just living out their lives in semiretirement.

She crossed to the small linen closet by the pantry and pulled out several dish towels. After wetting them down, she put them in the freezer.

"Don't ask," she said when Maribel looked at her. "I have a plan."

"Okay. Are you going to tell me what it is?"

"Not until I'm sure it works."

Carly didn't know if her friend knew about the ghost scam, but she didn't want to talk about it. She figured the fewer people who knew what was going on, the better.

After putting the still steaming muffins into several baskets, she carried them into the dining room.

It was midweek, so the B and B wasn't all that full. There

was one management off-site for a company that made some type of hoses. She hadn't been able to figure out if these were for the garden, cars or other things. She left a basket of muffins on their table, then crossed to the older couple in the corner.

"Morning, Mr. and Mrs. Abelson," she said brightly. "How are you enjoying your stay?"

"It's all wonderful," Mrs. Abelson told her as she patted her husband's hand. "Frank and I think this place is simply charming."

"Thank you."

The Abelsons were celebrating their forty-seventh wedding anniversary. Carly envied the obvious affection between them and the way they still held hands. Good to know that some marriages lasted.

She headed for the last table, where her mother leaned so close to Adam that she was practically in his lap. He seemed to be handling it all with an easy confidence that convinced her there was no point in feeling badly for him.

"Fresh muffins," she said as she set the basket on the table. "How is everything?"

Adam looked at her. "Great. Are you joining us?"

"No. I have some work I need to get to. But you seem well occupied."

Rhonda patted his arm. "We're keeping Adam entertained, aren't we, Tiffany?"

The teen giggled.

Rhonda glanced at Carly. "Adam was telling us he's not married. Isn't that interesting?"

As the older woman seemed to want him for herself, Carly wasn't sure whether the information was supposed to inspire or impress.

"It's great," she said, going for cheerful and not sure if she got there. "Huh, maybe I should look at a singles' event for the B and B. Something to think about."

She smiled and headed out of the dining room. After pouring herself a mug of coffee from the carafe by the registration desk, she walked toward her office, all the while trying to figure out plans to defeat Adam Covell. There had to be a way to convince him there was still a ghost in residence.

When she entered her office, she carefully closed and locked her door behind her. She didn't want Adam strolling in as she went over the papers and notes on how other eager ghostbusters had been fooled. Of course not many of them had come equipped with thermal imaging systems.

There were the misters, she reminded herself. After the towels she'd tossed in the freezer froze, she would take them into the crawl space and wrap them around the misters. The sudden burst of supercold air would give the imagers or whatever they were called, something to photograph.

Rearranging the furniture was a must, of course, but how to get around the system?

She glanced at her watch and then reached for the phone. With luck Jack wouldn't have left for school yet.

He picked up on the first ring. "Hello?"

"Jack? It's Carly Spencer, Tiffany's mom. Do you have a second?"

"Sure. What's up?"

She told him about Adam's background and all the equipment.

"Man, I hope he lets me see it," he said.

Carly smiled wryly. "I'm guessing all you'll have to do is ask. He's very approachable. But try to remember you're on our side."

"I know. Sorry."

"So how do we get around this stupid thermal imaging system? I want to rearrange the furniture without being caught. But if he can measure body temperature, we're in trouble."

Jack chuckled. "Not necessarily. Did you ever see a movie called *The Thomas Crown Affair?*"

"The first one or the second one?"

"There were two?"

"Yeah. The first one was before my time, too. You're talking about the one with Pierce Brosnan."

"Yeah. In it he uses a heater to raise the temperature in a room until it reaches body temperature. That way anyone moving around would be invisible."

"I love it!" she told him. Talk about clever. "I'll get to work on that right away." With the separate heating and cooling system for that room, she wouldn't even have to have a maid put in a heater.

"Well, could you wait to heat up his room when I can help?"

"Sure. I appreciate it, Jack. You're brilliant."

"Thanks, Mrs. Spencer."

She hung up and smiled. They were going to win this one, she told herself. High-tech equipment or not, they would have Adam Covell on the run.

CHAPTER 10

Carly pressed along the molding by the last door on the third-floor hallway. She heard a click, then felt something release. A concealed door swung open, showing her a narrow staircase leading up about six stairs.

"Okay, this is creepy," she muttered to herself.

"Go on," her mother said from her position behind her. "You'll be fine."

Easy for her to say, Carly thought. She wasn't the one climbing into total darkness. Still, it had to be done.

She clutched her flashlight in one hand and the plastic bag filled with frozen dish towels in the other and started up the stairs. At the top she turned and looked back at the open door. Some of her tension eased when she saw a release mechanism. At least she didn't have to worry about getting trapped in between floors. While she didn't think she had a problem with claustrophobia, this was not how she wanted to find out.

At the top of the stairs, the ceiling closed in. She crouched down and started crawling between joists. Up ahead light spilled in from a series of small windows. It was dusty and quiet up here, but she didn't smell anything icky, or hear rustling. Thank God. Seeing a mouse—or worse, a rat—would send her over the edge.

A narrow pipe snaked along beside her. Carly followed it until it stopped by a simple lever. When she bent closer to the pipe, she saw little nozzles at the end and a crack that allowed her to peer down into Adam's room.

"Found it," she called back to her mother, careful to keep her voice low even though Adam had left to go into town less than twenty minutes ago.

"Do you need any help?"

Carly glanced around at the cramped quarters. "I'm fine."

She pulled the still-frozen towels out of the bag and wrapped them around the pipe. Once that was done, she sat there staring at her handiwork. Okay, so how long would it take the frozen towels to chill the pipe?

"What do you think?" she asked. "Ten minutes?"

"That should do it."

Carly made her way back to the hallway where she and

her mother paced until the appropriate time had passed, then Carly returned to the secret passage and the hopefully chilled pipes. She pressed down once on the lever.

A definite *hiss* filled the silence. So some sort of mist had drifted into Adam's room. About five seconds later she heard a faint beeping coming from equipment below.

Not knowing if the sound was good or bad, she quickly unwrapped the pipes, then scurried back to the hallway.

"Something happened," she said. "He's got beeping machines."

"Good. They probably picked up the sudden drop in temperature."

Carly hoped that was the case. But with Adam being so into the whole science thing, she wasn't sure the mist trick would fool him.

"We're going to have to find a way to get him out of the house for longer," Carly said. "Heating the room up to body temperature has to be done slowly. Jack thinks we need at least two hours to heat it and two hours to cool it off. I wish I knew of some event he wanted to attend. But he hasn't mentioned anything."

"I invited him to join us for dinner tonight," her mother said. "We can talk about it then."

Carly shoved the still-frozen towels into the plastic bag. "Why did you invite him to dinner?"

"He seems like a nice man. He's alone. I was being polite."

"He's trying to ruin us. If he's successful, there's no way I can make the B and B pay. We'll have to sell."

Her mother shrugged. "I'm sure that won't happen. My point is during dinner we can find out if he has any interests and then suggest things in the area he might like."

Carly didn't actually object to Adam joining them for dinner; she just thought it was strange for her mother to ask. Still, he was pretty enough to look at that she would enjoy the distraction.

"If we can't get him to go bird watching or something, maybe we can convince him to go to San Francisco," Carly said. "His home address is in Virginia. Maybe he's never been to this coast before."

"We'll have to ask that, too," Rhonda said. "Now you go freshen up for dinner. You'll want to look your best."

Carly glanced at her watch. It was barely one in the afternoon. Even *she* didn't need that much time.

She closed the hidden door and made sure it latched in place, then excused herself to go to her office.

"I'm going to work for a while before I tackle the 'freshening up,'" she said.

"If you think that's wise." Her mother waved her fingers and headed toward the stairs.

It wasn't enough that Adam threatened their livelihood. Apparently he also threatened their sanity, something already in short supply around here.

Despite her best intentions to ignore the impending meal with Adam, Carly found herself in her bedroom a half hour before dinner. With her mother in charge of the cooking, there was little for Carly to do but show up. Or in this case, stare at herself in a mirror and wonder where the lines around her eyes had come from.

She needed a facial, she thought, as she leaned close and pressed her fingertip against the skin over her cheekbones and around her jaw. Or maybe just a new face. Her complexion looked dull and blotchy. Honestly, in the past few weeks, she'd reduced her morning and night beauty routine to face washing, some eye cream and a moisturizer with a built-in sunscreen.

"What's up with my eyelashes?" she asked as she studied the thin, pale hairs. Didn't she used to have more of them?

Her eyebrows were okay, she thought as she picked up tweezers and pulled out a few stray hairs.

She glanced down at the faded T-shirt she wore over

jeans and decided she didn't want to deal with her body right now. Better to just be depressed about her face and let it go.

After she'd showered and washed her hair, she returned to her room, where she passed over her jeans for a pair of black slacks and a nice blouse. After blow-drying her hair—using a round brush to give it a little volume—she opened her makeup bag and pulled out a bottle of base.

"Let's see if I remember how to do this," she murmured.

Ten minutes later, she'd applied base, blush and powder and done her eyes. Three coats of mascara seemed to plump up her skimpy lashes. She slipped on the two-tone hoops she'd always liked and grabbed her watch. A pair of casual sandals completed the look.

Telling herself she *hadn't* gone to all this trouble for Adam wasn't something she could actually make herself believe. Okay, maybe she had, but it was more for the practice than anything else. Looking at Adam was like looking at those huge, expensive Lladró pieces. The ones that took up an entire table. Sure they were stunningly beautiful and everyone had a fantasy about owning one, but they weren't something everyone could afford.

But she could window-shop.

She took the front stairs down and walked into the main foyer. Jack was already there, his arm around Tiffany. Adam stood by the bottle of wine her mother had left on a tray. He saw her and smiled in a way that made her bare toes curl ever so slightly. She moved toward him, but before she could actually get there, the front door opened and Steve Everwood walked in.

Several things occurred to Carly at once. First, she didn't care if it was against the law and that she would go to prison—she was going to kill her mother for this. Second, that she was more disappointed than was reasonable, and third, talk about the makings for an uncomfortable evening.

"Carly," Steve said warmly as he moved toward her. "Thanks for asking me over to dinner."

As she hadn't issued the invitation, she could only smile at him, even when he took her hand in his, leaned close and kissed her cheek.

Tiffany made a choking sound, which pretty much summed up what Carly felt.

"Mr. Everwood just kissed my mother," Tiffany said in a not-so-low voice. "I'm going to die."

Steve grinned at her daughter. "That's as far as it's going, kid. You can relax."

Tiffany wrinkled her nose. "It's still gross. So if I don't tell anyone what I saw, can I skip the next exam?"

"Sure. If you want to get an F." He winked at Tiffany. "Kissing moms isn't against the law."

"It should be."

Steve chuckled, then turned to Adam. "Hi. We haven't met. I'm Steve Everwood."

Adam glanced from him to her. Carly didn't know what to say or why she felt compelled to explain anything.

"Mr. Everwood, ah, Steve, is a math teacher at the high school," she told Adam. "In fact he was my math teacher when I went there."

As the words spilled out of her mouth, she desperately tried to call them back. Tiffany shrieked.

"He was your *teacher?* We have the same teacher? And you're going out with him? Mo-om, you can't. It's all too weird."

Jack touched his finger to the tip of her nose. "Tiff, it's fine. They're both adults. They can have a mature relationship if they want."

"Says who?"

"Just go with it."

While Carly appreciated the *intent* behind the rescue, she wasn't sure she appreciated the actual rescue itself. She and

Steve weren't dating. Sure he'd asked, but she'd always said no. Currently the only one issuing invitations seemed to be her mother.

Rhonda walked in from the kitchen. She, too, had spent some time primping. She wore a silk blouse over black slacks and had curled her hair. Talk about twisted, Carly thought, when you figured they were both interested in the same guy.

"Oh, good," Rhonda said. "You're all here. Carly, don't make our guests stand. Everyone should go into the parlor. Or, since dinner's almost ready, let's move into the dining room."

She bypassed the large dining room used by their guests and led the way into the private, more formal room just next to the kitchen.

Carly took in the good china, the fine linens and the salads waiting on each plate and had the sudden suspicion that the reason she hadn't been asked to help with the cooking was that the meal had come from one of the restaurants in town.

Rhonda directed them to specific chairs. She claimed the one at the head of the table, with Adam on her right and Steve on her left. Jack sat opposite her, Tiffany sat next to Adam and Carly sat next to Steve.

Rhonda passed Adam a bottle of chilled chardonnay. "If

you wouldn't mind opening this for me. I'm not very good at these kinds of things. My late husband used to take care of things like that." She sighed softly, as if the pain of the moment nearly overshadowed any possible pleasure.

"I think I can manage it," he said as he took the corkscrew and went to work.

Steve turned to Carly. "Your mother sets a beautiful table."

"Yes, she does."

He glanced at the salad. "And she's a great cook."

"You bet. Wish I'd inherited that ability from her, but I'm into simple cooking."

"You do okay, Mom," Tiffany said. "Except that one time you tried to feed us duck. It was horrible."

"The duck or the thought of eating it?" Adam asked with a smile as he pulled the cork free and poured the wine.

"I never tasted it. How could I eat something I'd have as a pet?"

Carly agreed, but Neil had insisted she work on perfecting a recipe. He'd wanted fancy dishes served whenever he brought people from work home for dinner.

"You married?" Steve asked Adam.

"Divorced," he said easily.

Carly was surprised. She hadn't known that. Plus, he

was hardly old enough to have had that many life experiences.

"Really," she said. "Me, too."

"Steve's a widower," Rhonda said pointedly.

Carly got the momspeak message instantly. Death wasn't anyone's fault. Unlike divorce, which was a clear mark of failure.

"Guess we'll have to wear a scarlet *D* on our chest," Adam said with a wink.

"I'll have sweatshirts made up," she told him.

"What's with the *D?*" Tiffany asked.

"Like an A, in *The Scarlet Letter,*" Rhonda said.

"It's a book," Adam added, leaning toward the teen. "We had to read it back in high school. It's old and...well, boring."

Carly grinned. She hadn't enjoyed the story, either. "But serious literature. You had to give them that."

"English wasn't my thing," he admitted. "Now give me a couple of hours on the football field and I was happy."

She could imagine him playing. "I thought you were the science guy."

"That, too. But I kept it a secret. I didn't want anyone to think I was a nerd."

Unlikely, she thought. Not with that face and body.

"Jack plays football," Tiffany said proudly. "He's the quarterback."

"Backup," Jack said. "But I'll be a senior next year and I'm going to be first string."

"Good for you," Rhonda said. "It's important to do well in sports."

Carly looked at her mother. Since when? But she didn't want to get into it now, not when Adam kept looking at Steve and Steve kept glaring back.

"How long have you lived here?" Adam asked Steve.

"About twenty-five years. I came right out of college. Got my first job at the high school and liked it enough to stay. Where are you from?"

"Back east. I'm in Virginia right now, but I've moved a lot with my job."

"No roots, huh?" Steve asked, his tone implying a lack of roots was close to a felony. "Most people want to settle somewhere."

"I've never been all that interested in settling," Adam told him.

Carly glanced at her mother. Okay, this was getting out of hand. Rhonda looked worried and mouthed, "Do something."

Carly grabbed her wineglass. "I'd like to propose a toast. To friends, old and new."

The men stopped eyeing each other and joined in the toast. When the glasses had been set down on the table, Carly turned to Steve and asked with as much interest as she could summon, "You mentioned the new computer labs on campus. Tell me about them."

Dinner was long. Too long for a meal of salad, pasta and sorbet. Every time either Steve or Adam started to tell a story, the other interrupted with a completely unrelated topic. Tiffany laughed too much at one of Adam's jokes, which had made Jack sulk. Carly had found herself trying to occupy Steve to keep the peace, when she really wanted to listen to Adam. Not only did she not get what she wanted, she had a feeling she'd given Steve more encouragement than was safe. Her suspicion was confirmed when he stood and said he had to be going, then asked if she would walk him out.

"Sure," Carly said, her entire dinner forming a tight, hard knot in her stomach.

Once they walked out of the B and B, Steve moved close and took her hand. Just like that. She did her best to relax and tried not to think about how long it had been since a man other than Neil had touched her that way. But it was difficult to stay calm when she was busy trying not to hyperventilate.

"Thanks for asking me over," he said, as if unaware of her panic. "You turned me down so many times, I figured you weren't interested."

She glanced at him and forced a smile. The man was being nothing but nice. It was hardly his fault she'd forgotten how to interact with the opposite sex. "It's not that. Not exactly. Between settling Tiffany and making some changes around here, I've been running around like a crazy person."

"Are you going to have some time for yourself soon?"

Eek! How did she answer that? Steve seemed really nice. Was it his fault he didn't make her toes curl? Wouldn't she be an idiot not to find out if she liked him? Not that she was interested in anything serious. At least she didn't think she was. Around Adam, Steve wasn't all that thrilling, but by himself he wasn't so bad.

"I can probably sneak away for a couple of hours," she said, then instantly wondered if she should have.

"Then I'll definitely call this week."

"Great."

They paused by his car—a black sedan. He released her fingers and put his hands on her shoulders.

Oh. My. God.

He was going to kiss her. She could tell by his intent gaze and the way the corners of his mouth turned up in anticipation. A kiss. Yikes! Did she want this? Did she want her first post-Neil kiss to be from her former math teacher?

Before she could decide or he could make his move, the front door of the B and B opened. Adam stepped out with Tiffany and Jack. Light spilled onto the gravel parking lot.

Carly instantly stepped back and folded her arms over her chest. "Okay. Well, this was great. Thanks for coming."

Steve looked at the trio, then back at her. "Next time," he promised.

She smiled but didn't speak. What was there to say? She didn't know what she felt or what she wanted, except possibly more wine.

She walked toward the front of the B and B, then turned to wave as Steve drove away. Tiffany and Jack wandered off toward his car—where Carly was sure there would be a whole lot more going on. As she walked by Adam, he grabbed her arm.

"Did I interrupt anything?" he asked. "Should I apologize?"

"No, on both counts."

His fingers burned her through her blouse and made her want to throw herself at him. Oh, yeah, definite tingles, she thought. Now why couldn't that happen with Steve?

She pulled free and walked into the house. Apparently

getting older didn't mean getting smarter—at least not where men were concerned.

"Dad wants to see me," Tiffany announced as she danced into Carly's office late on Thursday. "He's coming to San Francisco and I need you to drive me there. It's so cool, because I only have a half day at school tomorrow. He's getting in around two and we can meet him there just after. We're staying at a hotel and I have my own room."

Carly looked up from the ads she'd been approving. "Sounds exciting," she said, pleased that Neil had finally come through. Although he'd gotten better at the phone calls, it had been nearly three months since he'd seen his daughter.

"It is. Oh, Dad said he'd drive me back so you don't have to worry about that. He said we're going to the wharf and there's like a whole Ghirardelli chocolate-factory place. Isn't that the best?"

"I think you'll have a great weekend. I'm glad."

Tiffany spun in the center of the room, then came to a stop. "I don't have anything to wear. None of my clothes are right for San Francisco. We have to go shopping."

"I don't think so. You have lots of pretty things. Plus I bought you several new things when we moved here."

"But I've worn them all."

"And you can wear them again. No one in San Francisco has seen them."

Tiffany puffed out her lower lip. "You're not a lot of fun anymore," she said.

"Tell me about it. But I have an idea. We'll trade. I'll go to school, hang out with your friends and spend the weekend away. You can stay here and run the B and B and deal with Grandma. Then we'll see who is the most fun."

Tiffany ignored that. "Where's the luggage?"

"In the storeroom. But before you lose yourself in packing, I want you to finish your homework. Somehow I doubt you'll get to it this weekend."

"Oh, Mo-om. You worry too much."

"You don't worry enough. Homework," she said, pointing to the door. "I'll get your suitcase out and give it to you after you're finished."

Tiffany rolled her eyes, then turned and left. Her step was decidedly less bouncy on the way out.

Carly waited until she was gone, then stood and went in search of her mother. Was this trip to San Francisco the break they'd been looking for with Adam? They needed to get him out of the house for a few hours so they could work on rearranging the furniture in his room.

So far, he hadn't said anything about the misting incident, but based on his opinion of the whole paranormal phenomenon, she doubted it had convinced him.

She found her mother in the kitchen, checking their wine inventory.

"We need more chardonnay," Rhonda said as she counted bottles in open cases. "It's our most popular wine."

"I'll put a call in to the rep," Carly said. She'd recently acquired a wine rep who took their orders, then had the wine delivered. Not only did they get a better selection than that offered at the local discount store, but she was able to take advantage of winery incentives.

"Neil called Tiffany," she said. "He's spending the weekend with her in San Francisco."

"Oh, that's nice. She needs to be with her father more. A man's influence is so important."

Carly had several thoughts on the subject, the first being she didn't think Neil was all that great an influence, be he male or not. However, that wasn't the point.

"I'm driving her to the hotel tomorrow afternoon. She only has a half day at school. It's a couple of hours there and a couple of hours back. I thought I'd ask Adam to come with me."

Rhonda blinked at her. "Adam? Why would you do that?"

"So you can raise the temperature in his room. I'll call Jack and see if he can come in to rearrange the furniture."

"I don't see why you're the one spending the afternoon with Adam," Rhonda said with a sniff.

Insanity ran in the family. Carly had always wondered and now she knew for sure.

"Okay. Fine. You take Tiffany into town and drop her off with Neil. Then you can take Adam with you and hang out together."

Her mother's gaze narrowed. "Now you're being ridiculous. Why would I want to do that?"

Because you're acting like a jealous lover! Carly wanted to shriek the words aloud, but she held back. Adam made them all crazy. There was something about the guy that twisted female minds in a very unflattering way.

"I'm open to either scenario," she said honestly. "Maybe you'd enjoy the trip to the big city."

"I don't want to see your ex-husband. No, I'll stay here. You go."

The last two words were uttered on a very long sigh. Payment to follow, Carly thought, knowing there was no way around it.

"Just call before you come back," Rhonda told her. "If we're not done, you can stall him."

Carly wasn't sure how she was supposed to stall Adam, but she would deal with that issue at the time.

"Okay. I'll go ask him if he wants to go."

"He's out by the cliffs," her mother offered helpfully.

"Thanks."

Carly walked out of the house, toward the ocean. As she saw Adam sitting on a bench, facing the water, she slowed her step. Talking about asking him to join her in the city was one thing. Actually doing it was another.

What excuse could she give? How did she phrase it? Would he take the invitation wrong? Okay, unless he suspected her of trying to get him out of the house so they could do their best to trick him into thinking there was a ghost, then probably not.

"Hi," she called as she approached.

He looked at her, then smiled a slow, seductive smile designed to make her knees go weak. It worked, too.

"Hi, yourself. What's going on?" he asked.

"Not much."

She paused by the bench and looked out at the vast Pacific. The water was flat—a sheet of blue and green and gray that stretched out as far as the eye could see. Whatever else might go wrong in her life, at least this was always right.

She wasn't sure how to open the conversation. Should

she talk about the invitation? Hint? Only he couldn't possibly get a hint, so it was probably best to just jump right in.

"I'm taking Tiffany to San Francisco tomorrow," she said, staring at the view rather than at him. "She's spending the weekend with her father. I thought maybe you'd like to come along. After I drop her off, we could look around the city some."

He stunned her by grabbing her hand, which forced her to look at him.

"I'd like that," he said. "We could have dinner down by the wharf. It's one of my favorite places."

"Oh, you've been before?"

"Lots of times."

She was pretty impressed that she was able to form an entire sentence, what with his thumb brushing against her fingers. Back and forth, back and forth. She felt both tingles and heat. And they were climbing up her arm and heading for other, more interesting, body parts.

Oh, no, she thought as she pulled her hand free of his. No way was she going to get all attracted to him. Talk about a disaster. He wasn't her type—not that she'd figured out her type yet, or even if she wanted one. Either way, it wasn't Adam. He was too…too…

"How old are you?" she asked before she could stop herself.

"Thirty-three."

She'd known he was younger, but she'd hoped he was one of those guys who just aged really well.

"I'm forty. That's seven years," she said, watching him closely so she could see him flinch. She figured a good flinch or recoil would take care of her tingly issues.

"Okay."

She waited, but that was all he said.

"That would make me older than you. Seven years older. I have a teenage daughter."

He grinned again, and damn if her knees didn't get all weak and bendy.

"I can do simple math," he said in a mock whisper. "Kind of goes with the rocket scientist thing. And I still want to have dinner with you."

"Fine. Then we'll have dinner. We're leaving about two-thirty."

"I'll be ready."

She nodded tightly and walked back to the house. Her body felt hot and parts were more damp than they should have been. She waited until she was safely inside before stomping her foot. She would not, *not*, be attracted to this man. Her only interest in him lay in convincing him there was a ghost in residence. Aside from that, he didn't exist.

She would hate every minute of their time together. It would be slow and painful and probably boring, because, seriously, what was there to talk about with someone that young?

More important, she thought, as she crossed to the elevator and pushed the up button so she could go to her room, what was she going to wear?

CHAPTER 11

Neil had chosen a relatively inexpensive hotel a couple of miles north of the wharf. While Adam graciously agreed to drive around the block to save them from the hassle of finding parking, Carly walked her daughter into the foyer and used the house phone to call for Neil.

Her ex-husband came down immediately. Tiffany launched herself at her father and started to cry. Carly chose to take a more impersonal approach.

As father and daughter embraced, she studied the man she'd married. In some ways, he was intimately familiar. She knew every inch of his body, from his thinning reddish-brown hair to the birthmark on his right instep. She'd loved him, hated him, fought with him, cooked for him, made love with him and thought she was building a future with him.

"Hi," he said as he released Tiffany, who clung instead of letting go.

"Neil." She probed her heart, searching for some feelings, but there didn't seem to be any left. Could she really already not care?

"Want to see her room?" he asked. "I did what you said—got her the one next to me. It's got two double beds and everything."

"I'm sure she'll be fine."

If she wasn't, Tiffany had the number to the house and wouldn't hesitate to call.

"Have a good time," she told them, gave her daughter a quick kiss on the cheek, then walked out of the hotel. Even as she wondered if she should stay and talk, she reminded herself that she and Neil had run out of things to say a long time ago. Better that he and Tiffany reconnect.

She found Adam waiting, his rented SUV double-parked. She climbed into the front seat.

"Go okay?" he asked as he pulled into the street and headed up the hill.

"Fine. I hope Tiffany has a good time."

"I'm sure she will. What about you? Are you looking for a good time, too?"

Despite the teasing tone to his words, Carly felt her stomach tighten. She wanted to scream that, yes, yes, she was very interested! Extremely interested. Good time, bad time, just so long as they were both naked and touching everywhere.

As stunned by the thought as by the graphic images that accompanied it, she cleared her throat before speaking. "I, uh, have always enjoyed the wharf and Pier 39. Want to start there?"

"Sure."

Forty minutes later they'd parked in one of the large structures across the street and were strolling along the pier. The scent of salt air mingled with grilling meat and fresh popcorn. It was a beautiful late May afternoon, and tourists crowded the area.

Two little girls ran toward them, their parents in hot pursuit. Adam grabbed her hand to pull her out of the way and when the family had passed, he didn't let go.

"Was it strange seeing your ex again?" he asked as he laced his fingers through hers.

Not as strange as this good-looking younger guy holding her hand, she thought, determined to act as if this was completely normal and happened to her all the time.

"Not so much strange as sad. We were together for a

long time and now all that is gone. Except for Tiffany, it feels like a waste."

"Do you miss him?"

She glanced at Adam, who was staring out at the water.

"No. I don't love him. I haven't in a really long time. Plus, even if I did have some things to get over, the B and B has given me plenty of work to keep me busy and time to think. There's nothing like an afternoon of folding laundry to clear the mind."

"I'll have to try that sometime," he said with a chuckle.

"Oh, sure. Like that's ever going to happen."

"The house has been in your family a long time," he said.

"Nearly a hundred and fifty years. I can't imagine a world without it. I grew up there and it was a great childhood. So much space, interesting people coming and going. I didn't have to go into the world, it came to me."

"So why did you leave?"

She glanced at him. "You're asking a lot of questions."

"I'm interested."

Gee, when was the last time a man had said that to her? "Okay. But only because you asked. I left when I grew up. I wanted to see the world for myself. I moved to L.A. with my friend Maribel."

"The cook who makes the fabulous scones and muffins?"

"That's her. We were going to make our mark on the world. She lasted three weeks, then went back and married her high school sweetheart and started having babies. I went to college for a couple of years, then got a job planning events. Mostly big Hollywood parties and movie premieres. A lot of fun, but tons of pressure."

"When did you give it up?"

"When I had Tiffany. There were a lot of late hours and I didn't want to be gone from her. I tried wedding planning, but that meant being gone every weekend, so I ended up managing a doctor's office. After the divorce, I came back here."

"Are you glad you did?"

"Some days." She hesitated.

He pulled her over to the railing and stared into her eyes. "What?" he asked. "What aren't you telling me?"

"That the business isn't doing that well. It was in trouble when I arrived and I'm doing everything I can to make it successful. We're rebuilding our regulars and trying new things, like management seminars and off-sites and having special groups in. I have some horror writers coming in a few weeks and several culinary weekends and weeks. I'm trying to book a few weddings, some big parties, that sort of thing."

"How's it going?"

"Pretty well." He was so close, she could feel the heat of his body. "The thing is, our ghost is a big draw. Without that, we're just some old house on the coast in an out-of-the-way place."

"You need Mary to be successful."

"Exactly."

His dark gaze never wavered. "Then I hope she's real."

And she had been hoping for more. Like an agreement to stop trying to prove Mary wasn't. Of course that didn't make any sense. Adam didn't owe her anything.

He shifted a little closer. They weren't exactly touching, but it was a near-miss. She could feel his chest just millimeters from her breasts, and any second now his thighs were going to brush against hers.

"Who ended the marriage?" he asked.

"What?"

"You and Neil. Who ended things?"

"Oh. Um, he did. He left to go find himself."

"Was he lost?"

Carly laughed. "Apparently. Neither of us had been happy for a while, but I didn't think that was a reason to leave. I thought 'forever' really meant that. He didn't. I tried to tell myself that him leaving me to search for himself was better than him leaving for a younger woman, but I'm not so sure."

"He'd be crazy to leave you for someone else."

"As we discussed earlier, I'm forty."

"So? You make forty look good."

Man, oh, man did he have a way with words. "Thanks."

"I'm not kidding. You're amazing."

She felt the trembling start and knew it was a really bad idea to let things go any further so she slid a little to the left and turned to stare at the water.

"You mentioned you were divorced," she said, hoping she sounded more calm than she felt. "What happened in your relationship?"

"We didn't get along as well as we thought." He moved next to her and rested his forearms on the railing. "We were both twenty-seven and all our friends were getting married, so we figured we should, too. Within a couple of months of the wedding, we knew we'd made a mistake. Rather than stay and make each other miserable, we split up."

As simple as that, she thought. "I guess not having kids helped keep things less complicated."

"Sure. Kids would have changed everything. We'd both wanted to wait on that. Maybe because deep down we weren't sure it was going to last."

"You have plenty of time to start a family," she said. Yet another reason it wouldn't work between them. He would want children and her reproductive system had already gone into semiretirement.

"I'm sure you'll meet someone," she told him, going for perky and positive.

"Me, too," he said with a meaningful tone that left her breathless…and terrified.

"So, um, where do you want to eat dinner?" she asked. "There are a lot of great restaurants around here. I guess we should think about dining early because it's a long drive back to the B and B."

He turned to face her and placed his hand on her forearm. "Do I make you nervous?"

What kind of a question was that? Was it reasonable? Was it fair?

"'Nervous' is strong," she said. "How about *uneasy?*"

"That's better?"

"I'm not sure if it's better, but it's different."

"Why?"

"Because they're not the same feeling. 'Nervous' is—"

He squeezed her arm. "No. Why do I make you uneasy?"

"It's a really long list and I'm not sure we have the time."

He gave her that slow, sexy smile. "I have all the time you need."

"See, that's one of the reasons. You say things like you just said. It's confusing."

"Because you don't know if I'm coming on to you or not."

He wasn't asking a question, which was good, because she wasn't about to answer even if he was. Jeez—was there anything he *wouldn't* talk about? She didn't remember the men in her life being this self-assured. Was it a generational thing? Or was it the difference between a guy at twenty-two and one over ten years older?

He leaned close enough to brush his lips against her cheek, which he did.

She'd barely had a chance to realize what he'd done when he shifted so that he could speak directly into her ear. "I am hitting on you."

The time between leaving the pier and heading over to the wharf to pick a restaurant for dinner passed in a blur. Carly was sure they'd walked and even talked, but she had little or no recollection.

No doubt the combination of his light kiss and the claim that he was coming on to her had scrambled her perimenopausal synapses until they became disconnected or overloaded or whatever it was synapses did when they failed. When she resurfaced, she and Adam were being shown to a waterfront table by a cute twenty-year-old in a short skirt. The girl/woman gave Adam the once-over followed by a smile that offered more than good service at the restaurant.

"Nice place," Carly said as she picked up the menu, then set it down. Eating seemed impossible. As she wasn't driving, maybe liquor was the answer.

"It's one of my favorites. Everything is good here."

A waiter set a basket of bread on the table, along with a small cup of butter. Carly inhaled the faint scent of sourdough and thought about how her jeans could be tight by morning. She did her best to ignore the bread, while giving the waiter her drink order.

"Vodka tonic with a lime," she said. Usually she ordered it "tall" which meant more tonic and less vodka, but tonight she was going for false courage. Or at least enough of a buzz so she didn't actually care.

"You okay?" Adam asked after he'd ordered Scotch. "You've been quiet."

"I'm fine. I was just thinking we've been doing all this talking about me. What about you? Tell me about your work."

"Solid fuel science is mesmerizing," he teased. "I wouldn't want to tell you everything at once. It's like a great story—you have to draw it out."

"Now you're making fun of me."

"No. I'm pointing out that what I do is really interesting to me, but the rest of the world could easily sleep through the explanation."

Fair enough. She'd never been all that interested in the hows and whys of things. She just wanted them to work.

"It's a very specific specialty. How did you pick it?"

"It picked me. I was doing my postgraduate work in fuel cells, when a buddy asked me to help him with some experiments. I got hooked and had to change direction. Not something my parents wanted to hear, since I'd already been in college six years."

"You have a Ph.D.?"

"Two."

Of course he did. And she had those two scintillating years at a community college. They were practically twins, separated at birth. Not that she wanted to be related to Adam. That would mean her thoughts were not only inappropriate, they were also icky.

"Where do your parents live?" she asked.

"Arizona. Scottsdale."

"Oh, they're retired."

He shook his head. "My dad's only fifty-five. He's an engineer and works for an aerospace company out there. Mom has her own business, outsourcing payroll."

She supposed the good news was she was closer in age to him than his father, but still. Only fifty-five? She had friends that age.

"Your parents are really young," she said.

"You worry too much," he said. "So what if there's an age difference?"

"It's a big deal. We have nothing in common."

The waiter appeared with their drinks. Adam asked for a little more time before they ordered.

When they were alone, he picked up his glass. "We have more in common than you think. We want the same thing."

I… He… You…

Her brain shut down. She felt it and heard the audible click. One second there were thoughts, and the next—nothing. Not even a flicker of a concept.

"Carly?" Adam waved his hand in front of her face. "Are you okay?"

"Fine," she managed, then swallowed about a quarter of her drink.

"Did I say too much?"

"Oh, yeah. Don't do that again."

"So we should stick to nice, neutral topics and pretend this isn't happening."

She raised her glass and clinked it against his. "I'll drink to that."

* * *

As they walked back to the parking garage Carly was pretty pleased with herself. She'd survived dinner with Adam and it had actually been fun. He'd kept his word, so they'd talked about things like movies and places they'd traveled and family holiday traditions. She'd managed to keep her liquor to the single cocktail and a glass of wine, so while she felt a teeny, tiny buzz, she wasn't actually drunk.

Because drunk could be dangerous. Drunk could make her do things or want things or say things that could get her in a lot of trouble.

She wasn't sure if she was more worried that Adam would take her up on her offer or that he would be gentle and sweet as he turned her down. Both would be fairly hideous and she wasn't in a place where she could handle that kind of pain.

They entered the parking garage and headed for his SUV. Although he hit the remote to unlock the doors, he still walked around to her side of the vehicle.

But instead of opening the door, he stopped right next to her, cupped her face in both hands and kissed her. Just like that. No warning. Not even a hint.

Carly didn't know what to do. A strange man's lips were on hers. Everything was different—his height, his touch, his scent, even the way he gently brushed back and forth, slowly, ever so slowly.

She felt awkward. Her arms hung at her side. Was she supposed to touch him back? It had been too long since she'd kissed anyone but Neil. Apparently she'd forgotten what to do. How humiliating was that?

He raised his head and smiled at her. "How you doing?"

"Fine. Great. Peachy."

The smile grew into a grin. "Peachy?"

"Uh-huh. Probably not a word you've heard before. It's because I'm old. Older. Different vocabulary."

"I've heard peachy. Just not in this context."

He dropped his hands from her face to her wrists, grabbed her hands and put them on his waist.

"It would be nice if you liked this," he said quietly.

Pronouns exploded in her head again, but she ignored them. She ignored everything except the feel of soft cotton over his hard body. She pressed her fingers into his sides and met some seriously muscled resistance. This was a guy who worked out. Oh, yeah.

This time when he lowered his head to kiss her, she was prepared. Sort of. She closed her eyes and concentrated on the feel of his mouth against her mouth and allowed herself to get lost in the possibilities.

He wrapped both arms around her and drew her close, even as he angled his head and swept his tongue against her lower lip.

The unspoken request provoked an involuntary response. She parted for him. Even as she tried to accept the fact that they were touching *everywhere* from their shoulders and their thighs, she felt his tongue sweep inside.

Then they were kissing—seriously kissing. Something she hadn't done in the past until at least the second or third date. But they weren't dating, she reminded herself. And she wasn't seventeen anymore. So the hell with it.

She ignored the questions, the rules, the what-ifs and let herself drown in the sensations.

And boy, howdy, there were plenty. How his firm chest squished her breasts and made them ache, but in a really good way. How possessively he held her, as if he wanted to feel her, and keep her against him. The firm, yet gentle kiss that teased and aroused and made her wet and hungry.

Had kissing improved in the past twenty years or was Adam just really good at it?

Before she could figure out an answer, he drew back and looked at her. She liked the passion she saw flaring in his eyes, although she would have liked a little more proof that he was, well, interested. Despite the body pressing, she hadn't been able to feel, um, it.

"That was nice," he said as he brushed his fingers against her face.

"I thought so, too."

He kissed her cheek, then stepped back and opened the car door.

She climbed inside. The drive back was silent. Adam put in a CD and told her to close her eyes. She tried that, but every time she let her lids flutter closed she relived the kiss and she wasn't sure that was such a good idea. To her it had been fairly close to a life-changing event, but what had it been to him? No doubt he pretty much kissed every woman he met. He was young and gorgeous and she would do well to remember that he was just passing through.

"You're back late," her mother said when they stepped out of the SUV and walked up the front steps. Rhonda hovered by the front door, looking both annoyed and intrigued.

Adam smiled at her. "We had dinner on the wharf. Did I keep Carly out too late?"

"No. Of course not," Rhonda said, and playfully patted

his arm. "She's a grown woman. She practically has a grown daughter."

That made Carly wince. Tiffany was only fifteen, a long way from being grown.

He looked at her. "Thanks for inviting me. I had a great time."

"Me, too."

She wanted to say more, but what? Besides, her mother was right there, listening. He nodded at them both, then took the stairs two at a time.

Was he going to do that all the way to the third floor? she wondered, getting tired just thinking about it.

"What were you doing?" her mother asked in a low angry voice. "You were supposed to keep him occupied, not go gallivanting."

Carly took a step back. "We drove to San Francisco and dropped off Tiffany. Then we had dinner."

"I know how long it takes to eat a meal."

"What exactly are you accusing me of?"

Rhonda tugged at her shirt. "Nothing. I just don't want you to make fool out of yourself."

Great. "How did the furniture moving go? Did Jack come over?"

Rhonda hesitated, as if she wasn't going to accept the

change in subject. Then she spoke. "Yes, he was by. We moved the furniture around. Not a whole lot, but just enough for Adam to notice. It was incredibly hot in there."

"Good. We needed it to be body temperature. Has the room cooled off?"

"It should have. We'll see what Adam has to say about all this. I hope it convinces him."

"Me, too." Although she had her doubts. The man had two Ph.D. degrees. Was that fair?

Carly stretched. "I'm going up to bed, Mom. See you in the morning."

Instead of answering, her mother stared at her.

"What?" Carly asked.

"It's Adam, isn't it? You're getting involved with him."

"I'm not, but even if I was, what's the big deal?"

"He's too young for you."

Carly almost said "You, too," but held back. "There's nothing you have to worry about."

"But there is something?"

"No. There's nothing." Just a kiss and she wasn't going to share that with anyone else. "Night, Mom."

Unlike Adam, she took the elevator to the third floor, then walked to her room. Once inside, she pulled back the drapes to expose the night sky and the light of the moon.

Then she flopped back on her bed and stared up at the dark ceiling.

She wanted Adam. Sexual need filled her until she ached from the hunger. How long had it been since she'd felt that? The last two years of her marriage had been completely sexless. Oh, she and Neil had done it plenty of times, but she'd just been going through the motions. She hadn't experienced passion or desire. She hadn't felt anything.

She'd thought that it was her body changing, that as she got older, the hormones or whatever it was that created that sensation of desperate desire had simply dried up.

Apparently not. She was both restless and edgy.

She stood and walked back to the window where she pressed her hands against the glass in an effort to cool her body. How ironic that she'd had years of accessible sex and she hadn't been interested, but now that she didn't have a man around, she was hungry with longing. Wasn't that just always the way?

Was Adam interested? She wanted to think he was, but she wasn't going to test the concept with anything like an invitation. Besides, even if he wanted her in theory, reality was very different and possibly unpleasant.

There were stretch marks from her pregnancy, a few very

unattractive spider veins and old breasts. Seeing her naked could emotionally scar Adam for life, and she didn't think she could live with the guilt. Plus, once he'd seen her, he wouldn't be able to get it up and then where would she be? Depressed *and* unsatisfied.

Maybe a man closer to her age would be better. Someone like…Steve. He could—

Carly stared out at the darkness. She blinked twice as she turned the thought over in her head. Was she saying Steve was okay but Adam wasn't? But Steve was at least ten years older than she was and she was only seven years older than Adam. By her own definition, Adam was the better choice.

Except Steve was older and Adam was younger. Which meant she was giving in to sociological pressures that condoned an older man and younger woman but not the reverse. Which made her a hypocrite and just the sort of person she disdained and far too much like her mother.

Carly gave a soft laugh. She was also on the verge of going crazy. Apparently her mental heath was that tenuous. Sad, but true.

Well, the good news was that wanting sex as much as she did meant she was very much alive and hormonally healthy, if there was such a thing. She'd been kissed senseless by a very cool guy, and even if nothing else happened, she would also have that.

Now if she just had a ghost.

CHAPTER 12

Despite Carly's brave thoughts about the sociological unfairness of a society that trained women to believe that older men were more desirable by virtue of their age, if for no other reason, she did her best to avoid Adam for the weekend. As the B and B was full, staying busy and out of his way was amazingly easy. She made sure she worked hard enough on Saturday that she physically couldn't stay awake when she fell into bed that night and woke up bright and early Sunday to help Maribel with the brunch.

By four on Sunday, she was exhausted and wondering if she needed another plan. It didn't seem to matter how much she organized, cleaned, polished or planned, she couldn't stop thinking about Adam and their kiss. Worse, she'd wondered constantly if she was too old, too fat and too saggy to ever interest a man.

"Something I have to get over," she told herself as she finished proofing the ads she was sending off to two travel magazines. Not only didn't she have the time or energy to worry about that kind of stuff, it made her tired. She was forty—shouldn't she be able to accept herself for who and what she was?

She stuck the ads in the envelope, made a mental note to overnight them in the morning, then left her office to go hang out in the front parlor. Tiffany was due back any time now and Carly wanted to check in with Neil and make sure everything had gone well.

Fifteen minutes later, Neil drove up in his rental car and Tiffany bounced out of the passenger side.

"Hey, Mom!" she called as she ran up the front steps. "I'm back. Did you miss me?"

Carly hugged her daughter, then held her at arm's length to study her face. She had on a little more makeup than usual and her hair had been teased into a halo of semicurls, but otherwise she looked pretty much the same.

"It was very quiet without you," Carly said as she grinned at her daughter.

"I knew it would be. Oh, I bought you some bread."

Tiffany raced back to the car and danced impatiently

while her father opened the trunk. While he pulled out her small suitcase, Tiffany grabbed a bag and ran to the steps.

"It's this really big deal in San Francisco. They sell it everywhere. I had some at dinner last night and it's really good."

"Thanks." Carly took the bag and sniffed the delicious, fresh-baked, sourdough scent. Instantly her stomach rumbled.

Neil carried the suitcase to the steps and put it down. "Hey," he said. "We had a good time."

He sounded so surprised, Carly wanted to cuff him. If he'd spent more time with his daughter, he would know that when she wasn't being a typical teen, she was a great kid.

"I'm glad to hear that," Carly said. "What did you two do?"

Tiffany grinned. "We went to the wharf, and that pier place."

"Pier 39?"

"Yeah. And we took the trip out to Alcatraz. That was pretty cool, but kind of icky. Prison doesn't look as fun as it does in the movies. Oh, and Dad got me this. Isn't it so cool?"

As Tiffany spoke, she pulled up the hem of her T-shirt and exposed the small gold hoop in her belly button.

Carly felt her temperature climb about a hundred and

fifty degrees. Anger flared until she knew she could incinerate anyone in her path with just a glare.

"Tell me that's not real," she said in a low, harsh voice.

Tiffany gave a little shrug. "Dad said it was fine."

Of course he did, Carly thought, as she turned on her ex-husband.

"What were you thinking?" she demanded. "Neil, *we* agreed no body piercing until she was eighteen."

"I didn't agree to that," he said. "What's the big deal?"

She wanted to choke him. Right there, right that minute, she wanted to wrap her hands around his throat and squeeze the life out of him. But she didn't. Not only would it set a really bad example and possibly send her to prison, she didn't think she was physically strong enough to actually hurt him.

"It's a huge deal. We discussed the whole issue several times and we were concerned about what a pierced belly button said about Tiffany. You were totally on board with me. Neil, there are rules for a reason."

He simply looked uncomfortable and Tiffany looked so smug, Carly wondered if maybe not spanking her as a child had been a mistake.

Carly turned on her daughter. "This isn't over, Tiffany."

"I have it now and there's nothing you can do about it."

Want to bet? But Carly didn't say that. Instead she figured she might as well get all the bad news at once.

"Did you do the homework you were supposed to finish before and didn't?" she asked.

Tiffany smiled again. "Dad said I didn't have to."

"What?"

Neil winced. "I said it could wait, Tiff. Not that you could blow it off."

"You've got that right." Carly narrowed her gaze into the laser stare that always made her daughter uncomfortable. "Get upstairs right now and do your homework."

"But I don't want to."

"Do you think anyone here cares about that?"

Tiffany looked at her father. "Dad, tell her not to make me."

"No way." Neil took a couple of steps back. "You, ah, probably should have done it before."

Tiffany glowered at them both before sighing heavily, then grabbing her suitcase and heading inside.

When the front door closed behind her, Carly turned on Neil. "What the hell were you thinking? Dammit, Neil, this wasn't some teen movie you were playing in. You're Tiffany's father. You need to set an example and establish some rules. I know it seems really great to just be the buddy, but the only person that helps is *you*. In the end, Tiffany is left with an unrealistic picture of what the world will be and no skills with which to handle her life."

"You're such a drag," he muttered. "I took her. Isn't that good enough?"

He stood on the gravel, kicking at rocks, his hands shoved into his pockets. He looked closer to thirteen than forty-three, but without the little-boy charm.

"No," she said firmly. "It's not good enough. We have to present a united front. You had to know this was a bad idea."

"I don't get the kid thing."

"She is your *daughter*. Of your flesh. How can you not love her with every fiber of your being?"

"I love her."

The silent "sort of" echoed in her ears.

She didn't know how to get through to him. What combination of words would make him understand how important this was?

"You need to be her parent, not her friend. If you aren't willing to sometimes be the bad guy, you're hurting your daughter in more ways than you can imagine."

"Fine. Whatever. Are we done here?"

She'd never hated Neil before. Not when he'd disappointed her in their marriage, not when he'd told her he was leaving, not when she'd had to move out of her home and uproot Tiffany.

But she hated him now. She could excuse his actions within the context of their marriage, but she would never forgive him for refusing to give a hundred percent where Tiffany was concerned.

The front door opened and Adam stepped out.

After avoiding him for nearly two days, Carly had almost convinced herself that the attraction she felt wasn't real. But even in the middle of her rage, she was able to appreciate his lean good looks and how his smile made her heart beat faster.

"Am I interrupting?" he asked.

Neil jumped forward. "No. Not at all. I was just heading out." He frowned. "Adam, right? Tiffany mentioned you."

"Right."

The two men shook hands. Neil glanced between Adam and Carly.

"He's staying here?" he asked, as if not sure how to put the puzzle pieces together.

"He's here because of Mary," Carly said, knowing that Neil was now off the hook and would make his escape while there was a third party around to offer protection.

"Mary?"

"The ghost," Adam told him.

Neil rolled his eyes. "You're not still peddling that dumb story, are you?" He turned to Adam. "She loves that ghost. Thinks she's real. She has all these stories from when she was a kid and Mary was there. What a bunch of crap. Who believes in ghosts these days?"

"I do," Carly said icily, suddenly anxious to have him gone. She pointedly glanced at her watch. "Unless you want to talk about Tiffany some more, you should probably be going."

"What? Okay. Sure. Oh, I told Tiffany I'd see her in two weeks. I won't get the boat until the middle of next month, so I have time."

Great. Wow—everyone should be so thrilled about Neil's commitment to his daughter.

"You're buying a boat?" Adam asked with obvious interest.

"Yeah. A sailboat. She's real sweet, completely updated. I'll have to get in a better nav system, but that's about it."

"Neil's planning to sail to Hawaii," Carly said cheerfully.

Adam looked at the other man. "You have an understanding employer."

"Oh, he doesn't work," Carly said. "He's trying to find himself and a job gets in the way."

Neil narrowed his gaze. "It's not like that."

"Really? What's it like?"

Before he could answer, two cars pulled into the parking lot. Carly recognized them both. Jack showing up presented a minor problem, what with Tiffany about to be grounded, but Steve was a whole other issue.

Why was he here? She didn't think her mother had invited him over, which meant he'd decided to show up all on his own. Great—her ex-husband, the guy who had kissed her socks off and her former math teacher who might or might not be interested in her, all on the same porch. It was a very special moment.

Neil turned toward the cars. "Is that Jack? Tiffany talked about him all weekend. He seems like a nice enough kid, but I want to talk to him. If he and Tiffany are going to date, then he has to respect her."

Carly resisted the need to stick her finger in her ear and wiggle it around. "They don't date."

Neil looked at her. "Sure they do."

"Uh, *no*. They don't. She's too young and she knows that. No car dating. My God, she's only fifteen."

Jack walked up the stairs. "Hi," he said, nodding at Carly and Adam.

She drew in a deep breath. "Neil, this is Jack, Tiffany's friend. Jack, this is Tiffany's father."

Jack stiffened, then held out his hand. "Hi, Mr. Spencer. Nice to meet you."

Steve walked up the stairs and grinned. "Are we having a party?"

"Seems that way," Adam said, eyeing the other man. "What brings you out here?"

Steve put his arm around Carly's shoulders and pulled her in close. "Just being neighborly."

Carly felt everyone's attention on her. Neil looked both shocked and hurt, which once again gave her ideas about strangling him. Not that there was anything going on between her and Steve, but so what if there was? Neil had been the one to walk out on the marriage.

"Okay," Carly said, moving away from Steve, "time out. This is getting too complicated." She turned to Neil. "I'm glad you want to see Tiffany again in two weeks. I think it's great. But between now and then, you and I have to talk about ground rules."

"You're so uptight, Carly," her ex said. "You gotta loosen up."

"Where my daughter is concerned, that will happen when hell freezes over. Speaking of which—"

She glanced at Jack who immediately moved down a step. "I didn't do anything."

"I know. But Tiffany is grounded, so you can't see her now and she's going to lose her phone privileges for a week." Carly wasn't sure what to say about him seeing Tiffany—Jack had been a big help on the ghost front. And he wasn't the one who had misbehaved. "I may let you come over some evening this week. I don't know."

Jack shifted uncomfortably. "Sure thing, Mrs. Spencer."

The teen glanced longingly at the house, then nodded at the adults and went back to his car.

"You're tough," Steve said with a smile. "Good for you."

Neil glared at him. "I'm outta here. I have a long drive back to L.A. in the morning."

"Goodbye," Carly said, knowing the only way she and Neil were going to have a meaningful conversation about Tiffany was if she, Carly, physically tied him down and tortured him until he listened. While the visual was pleasing, she hated that he was so unwilling to take a little responsibility.

Now there were only two guys and herself. Carly looked between them and wondered what she was supposed to say. Steve touched her arm.

"I guess I should have phoned first," he told her. "Life is complicated here."

"It is. Especially now."

"No problem. I'll give you a call in a couple of days and we can pick a time to go to dinner."

With Adam standing so close, she felt awkward. What was the correct response? What did *she* want to say? Nothing occurred to her, so in the end, she nodded lamely and watched him walk away.

Adam crossed his arms over his chest and leaned against the railing. "This is getting interesting," he said.

"Maybe for you, but I find everything about this situation a nightmare." She started to walk past him.

He grabbed her arm. "Carly, wait. I haven't seen you in two days."

"I know. I've been sorting some things out."

"What did you decide?"

"I haven't a clue."

"Maybe we should go to dinner sometime."

"Maybe."

"You could try to sound a little more enthused."

Probably, but the concept was beyond her right now. "I have to go deal with Tiffany."

"Okay. We'll talk later."

She wasn't sure if that was a promise or a threat. She nodded and walked into the house. It wasn't that she didn't want to be with Adam—of course she did. Except for his refusal to believe in Mary—which made sense, considering she liked everything about him. But there were difficulties. And right now her daughter was a priority.

She took the elevator to the third floor, then climbed the stairs to Tiffany's tower rooms. She knocked once and waited for a reply. When there wasn't one, she pushed the door open.

Tiffany sat in a chair by the window. She stared out at the view, although Carly doubted the beauty of the ocean was really on her mind. Her expression was closed and Carly had a feeling this wasn't going to go well. Which was fine with her—she was in the mood for a fight.

"You know better," she said, keeping her voice low. She might be ready to take her daughter on, but she always tried not to scream. "You were extremely clear on the rules and you disregarded them. Just as bad, you played your father against me. You took advantage of the situation for your own personal gain. I'm not only angry, but I'm deeply disappointed in you. I thought you were more mature, but I can see I was wrong."

Tiffany glared at her. Carly wanted to think the part about her being disappointed had made an impact, but she couldn't tell.

"I don't know what you're so mad about," Tiffany said.

"Really? From your perspective, you did everything right?"

"Dad said I could get my belly button pierced. Doesn't he get to make rules, too?"

"Not that one." Carly narrowed her gaze. "You went behind my back, then you acted as if I would be happy about it."

"I'm not going to feel bad," Tiffany said, coming to her feet. "Your rules are stupid."

"In your opinion."

"In everyone's opinion!"

"Not mine, and I'm the most important someone in your life." Carly moved closer to her daughter. "You're fifteen years old. While I'm interested in your opinion on some matters, this isn't one of them. You will follow my rules and you will pay the consequences for not doing so when you know better. You deliberately defied me, Tiffany. I won't stand for that."

"Yeah? What are you going to do about it?"

"I'm so glad you asked. First, I want you to take out the belly button ring right now."

"What?" The teen's eyes filled with tears. "No! You can't make me."

Carly shrugged. "You're right. I *could* call your father

back and have him and Adam hold you down so I can take it out myself. If that's what you'd prefer, let me know. Your dad is heading back to San Francisco and I'd like to catch him before he gets too far."

"You're mean."

"About this. Oh, yeah. Take it out, Tiffany."

"No."

Carly walked to the phone sitting on the nightstand. She picked it up and dialed Neil's cell number.

"Hi, it's me," she said when he'd answered. "I'm sorry to bother you, but I need your help with something."

"Here!" Tiffany thrust the belly button ring at her.

Carly took it and held in a sigh. She hadn't wanted to ever have this conversation with her daughter.

"What's up?" Neil asked. "Carly? Are you there?"

"I am. Never mind. Sorry to bother you. See you in two weeks."

"Okay. Bye."

She hung up the phone and turned back to her daughter. Tiffany stood with a tissue pressed against her belly button.

"I'll probably get an infection and die," she said dramatically. "Then you'll be sorry."

Carly ignored that. "Put some antiseptic on the holes," she said as she bent down and unplugged the phone.

Tiffany shrieked. "What are you doing?"

"Taking away your phone for a week. This one and the cell." She held out her other hand. "Give it to me or I'll get it myself."

Tiffany grabbed her backpack and held it to her chest. "No. You can't..." Her voice trailed off. She reached inside and pulled out the phone.

"I hate you," Tiffany said, her voice low and angry. Rage burned in her eyes. "I hate you."

Weariness settled over Carly. She took the cell phone and tucked it in her pocket. "Right now you're not my favorite person, either."

Carly put the confiscated phones in her office, then walked into the kitchen. It was time to set out the appetizers and wine. As her mother was off for the afternoon, it was up to Carly to take care of it.

She opened several bottles of red and white wine first, then poured herself a big glass of cabernet sauvignon. After drinking about a third of what she'd poured, she turned on the oven and got out the puff pastries Maribel had left for her.

Adam walked into the kitchen. Without saying anything, he walked to the sink, washed his hands, then took the covered plate from her and put the rest of the pastries on the cookie sheet.

"What are you doing?" she asked.

"Helping."

"Why?"

"You look like you could use some."

Did that mean *pathetic?* She wasn't sure she could stand that.

"You're dealing with a lot right now," he said.

"You noticed."

"Hard not to. I don't want to add to that."

"I appreciate that, but why do I know you're still going to?"

He shrugged and carried the cookie sheet over to the oven. "What's next?"

She set him to work cutting up cheese, while she diced fruit.

"I'm surprised Neil isn't a believer—in Mary," he said.

"For a man who worked in advertising for twenty years, he has a surprising lack of imagination."

"Is that required for someone to believe in ghosts?"

"No. Seeing one can make even a cynic a believer."

He looked up from the cheese. "I've never seen one, Carly. And while I appreciate the effort you're making, it's not working."

She froze, knife poised to slice through a papaya. "What does that mean?"

He gave her a smile that could only be interpreted as tender, which, under any other circumstances, she would have appreciated.

"Raising the temperature in my room so the thermo-imaging wouldn't read the people rearranging the furniture was original. I give you full points for that. I keep a temperature monitor in my room. I know how fast it went up and back down again. I also have a motion-activated video-tape set up. It caught the whole thing."

Carly felt her cheeks flush. A camera. So he'd seen everything.

"The misting was interesting. How did you get it so cold?"

"I don't know what you're talking about."

He put down the knife and circled around until he stood next to her. "I like you a lot. I think I made that clear when we were in San Francisco. You're sexy as hell and I won't deny that I'd like to do something about it. But this isn't personal. It's about science and how the universe works. There are no ghosts."

"You're wrong," she said, feeling weak at the knees, and not because he stood so close. This was about watching her life disintegrate right before her eyes.

"I wish I was," he said as he touched her cheek. "I don't want to do this to you."

But he would. Because that was his job, or at least his hobby.

"You should go," she said as she stepped away from him.

"Are you asking me to leave the kitchen or the house?"

"Just the kitchen." There was no point in him leaving the B and B until she was able to convince him to keep quiet about the place or make him believe in Mary.

"Okay."

He bent down and kissed her cheek. She did her best not to react to the physical sensation, but apparently her body had already hardwired itself, where Adam was concerned. Every nerve went on alert and parts of her were very interested in something more physical.

She ignored the sensations of need and hunger and turned her back on him. After a couple of minutes, she heard him walk out of the kitchen. Only then did she move to a chair and collapse.

There had to be a way out of this. There *had* to be. Unfortunately she couldn't see what it was.

The group seemed less cohesive than it had before, less confident. Carly knew part of the problem was that Tiffany was still angry with her. They were only three days into the weeklong grounding, which would have been okay if Carly hadn't taken away phone privileges. She accepted that, for a teenager, not having a phone was close to death. But Tiffany had to learn there were consequences to her actions.

Rhonda was also there, but her interest in the fake-ghost project seemed to be wavering. Only Jack was excited and happy, no doubt because he got to spend some time with Tiffany.

"Adam wasn't convinced by anything we've done," Carly said when everyone had found a seat in the small, back parlor. She'd already closed and locked the door, just in case Adam returned from his walk early.

"Not even the furniture moving?" Jack asked.

"Nope. Apparently he had a video camera set up and saw the whole thing."

"Well, that's just ridiculous," Rhonda said angrily. "Isn't there a law against taking pictures of people without their permission?"

Carly shrugged, not sure how to answer the question. She figured there was no point in mentioning that going into Adam's room for the sole purpose of tricking him wasn't exactly aboveboard, either.

"We're going to have to come up with some other ideas," Carly told everyone. "Any suggestions?"

"We should just give up," Rhonda told her. "We tried and we weren't successful. We can make this place work without the ghost."

Carly shook her head. "We can't, Mom. I wish it were different. About seventy percent of the new bookings are because of the ghost. One of the culinary weeks is devoted to food from Mary's era. We can't make it on thirty percent of full. Without Mary, we're not worth visiting. If we give up, then we might as well simply close our doors and sell."

Jack looked stricken. "You'd do that?"

"We wouldn't have a choice."

He looked at Tiffany who seemed to be equally unhappy at the thought.

"There has to be something," her daughter said.

"I'm open to suggestions."

"Magnets," Jack said as he sat up straight in his chair. "Isn't Adam checking on electromagnet energy?"

"I think so."

"Then we can rent a big magnet—an industrial-size one. We can bring it up in the elevator, plug it in and turn it on. That will zap his equipment in a huge way." He paused. "It's going to be noisy, though. I think a magnet that big would require a generator. It couldn't run off house currents."

Carly saw the possibilities at once. "Why don't you take that one?" she said. "I think it's a great idea. Find out where we can rent one and all the stuff we need to make it work. But it can't be bigger than the elevator."

"Good point." He made a couple of notes.

Carly considered other options. "I wonder if there's a way to create cold spots in his room," she mused. "I'll look for that on the Internet. Maybe in some joke shops."

"Locks," Tiffany blurted. "Remote locks. We could activate them somehow and lock him in a room. Or out of it."

"That's great!" Carly said.

She grinned at her daughter, who smiled back until she remembered they weren't speaking. Then her smiled faded.

"Whatever," she said, sounding bored. "I don't really care what you do."

Jack leaned close to Tiffany. "It's a great idea."

She smiled at *him*.

Carly made some notes. "Okay, we have a new plan. Jack, you'll research the magnet and get back to me. Tiffany, how about looking for remoteactivated locks? I'll find out about cold spots. Mom—"

"I'll keep Adam occupied," Rhonda said. "I don't think you should spend any more time alone with him."

Carly felt both Jack and Tiffany turn in her direction.

"Fine by me," she said, and meant it. Right now her life felt plenty full. She wasn't sure she could handle one more thing, and Adam certainly qualified as that.

CHAPTER 13

As promised, Steve called and invited Carly to dinner. She wasn't sure if she wanted to go on an actual date with him, but she wasn't sure she didn't, either, so she'd accepted.

Now that she'd gotten used to the idea of him as a contemporary instead of a teacher, she could admit he was nice and funny and okay, while he didn't make her heart race or her body shake the way Adam could, he was still a fun guy. Sex wasn't everything, right?

Oh, who was she kidding? After the past few years of lackluster lovemaking with Neil, she felt she was due for something spectacular. So far, Adam seemed to be in the running for that—although she wasn't sure if she had the courage to give in if asked.

Steve...well, she wasn't so sure about him. Yes, he was attractive, but so far there hadn't been any tingles. Of course there hadn't been much chance for close encounters. She would have to see how the night went.

She ran a brush through her hair one more time, then gave herself a quick once-over. A pale summer dress skimmed her body to just above the knee. Her sandals were relatively new and purchased for their cuteness rather than their practicality. She debated bringing a sweater, then chose fashion over comfort and left it behind.

At exactly six twenty-nine she went downstairs and found Steve in the foyer, talking to Rhonda. He looked up as she entered and smiled at her.

"Hi," he said as he walked toward her. He paused at her side and kissed her cheek. "You look gorgeous," he murmured in her ear.

"Thanks."

He looked pretty good, too. Not as overtly handsome as Adam, but still appealing in a charming, older-man sort of way. She was happy to see him and looking forward to the evening. Both good signs.

Carly waved to her mother and walked out with Steve. When he held open the passenger door of his black sedan, she had the feeling of being watched from the house. She glanced back over her shoulder, half expecting, half hoping to see Mary at one of the windows. But there wasn't anyone. No person and no ghost. Maybe she should simply accept that Mary hadn't existed. As much as she wanted things to be different, they weren't and she should probably get used to that.

The restaurant Steve chose had once been a winery. There were still old barrels stored up in the rafters and the scent of grapes lingered in the paneling. They were shown to a quiet table in the corner where they had a view of the lush courtyard.

Steve ignored the menu and leaned toward her. "I've been looking forward to this for a while."

"Really?"

"Sure. I was intrigued that first day when you brought Tiffany to school."

"Oh, good. So I don't have to worry that you thought about me before that."

He grinned. "I'm not that twisted. A teacher thinking about a student? Not my style."

"Twisted? Interesting word choice."

"Hey, I learn plenty of hip talk in class."

She leaned close. "You know we don't say hip anymore, right?"

"I'd heard that. But I'd always liked the word."

She smiled. "Good to know." She fingered her menu but

didn't pick it up. "I was surprised you were still here. I know what you said about liking the town and putting down roots, but still. It's not the big city."

"I grew up in Chicago. When I graduated from Northwestern I had two goals—to never shovel snow again and to live near the ocean. I have both here. Then I got married and had kids. We didn't want to uproot them, and to be honest, I didn't want to uproot myself. I guess I could have had more ambition, but I don't."

Wanting a simpler life looked okay on Steve, she thought. "You make a difference," she said. "That matters more than ambition. You touch those kids every day."

"Not every day. Maybe once a week. When things are going well."

She laughed. "Fair enough. How old are *your* kids?"

"Brad, the youngest, is in his first year of college. The twins, Katie and Mark, graduate next year. She's going to be a kindergarten teacher and he's applying to law school."

She winced. "That's a lot to pay for."

"It's not a problem. Bonnie had a large life insurance policy. It's going to put the kids through college and then some."

"I'd heard your wife died. I'm sorry."

"Me, too. We had a great marriage. She was diagnosed

with liver cancer in September and gone before Christmas. In some ways it was easier that it was so fast. She suffered a lot less. Selfishly, I wanted her around a whole lot longer."

"I'm sure you did."

None of her friends had lost a spouse. That was supposed to happen to parents and friends of parents.

"How long has it been?" she asked.

"The kids were still pretty young. It was hard. Bonnie's mom moved in for a few years. People thought I was crazy asking my mother-in-law to come live with us, but she was terrific. She picked up the slack, gave Katie a woman to talk to and got us through the worst of it."

"Where is she now?"

"Enjoying her well-deserved retirement in Sun City. That's down south. She has a lot of friends there and it's close enough that we can all visit."

He shook his head. "This wasn't how the conversation was supposed to go. I was going to dazzle you with my wit and charm."

"What makes you think you haven't?"

He raised his eyebrows. "Then you have really low standards."

She laughed. "I don't get out much."

"Any dating since the divorce?"

"No." When would she have found the time? Plus there weren't exactly dozens of men lining up to spend the evening with her.

"So I'm the first?"

She nodded, knowing she couldn't really count her dinner with Adam. She'd invited him for the express purpose of getting him out of the house for the failed furniture rearranging. As for the kiss afterward, she wasn't thinking about it anymore, let alone talking about it.

"Speaking of living with relatives, how are you doing with your mom?" he asked.

Carly wrinkled her nose. "It's okay. Some days are easier than others. I'm sure Tiffany would say I make her as crazy as my mom makes me, but I can't imagine it."

"You're in a unique situation," Steve told her. "Your mother is a lovely person, but she's also a professional victim. No matter what happens, it's never her fault."

The waiter appeared just then and asked for their drink orders. Carly thought she'd asked for white wine, but she wasn't sure. She was too stunned to think.

Steve had nailed it. In two words, he'd summarized her mother in a way she'd never been able to do. Of course—a professional victim. That explained so much. Everything really.

"Are you all right?" Steve asked when the waiter had left.

"What? Oh, yes. I was thinking about what you said. You're so right—she *is* a professional victim. Why does being able to name the condition suddenly make it easier to deal with?"

"Not a clue," he said.

"Maybe it makes me feel I'm less crazy."

"Are you crazy?"

"Sometimes."

"Then I'm glad I could help."

Whatever concerns or tensions she'd had about the evening faded away. Suddenly she wanted to know everything about him.

"Okay, enough about me and my mother," she said. "What do you do for fun around here?"

Nearly two hours later Carly set down her fork and groaned. "I ate way too much. I'm going to have to make up for this by never eating again."

"I'm glad you liked everything," Steve said, looking amused.

"What?" she asked.

"I never thought you'd get through that whole slice of prime rib, let alone the banana cream pie."

She glanced down at her empty plate. "Yes, well, I was hungry."

"Apparently."

Oh, no. Had she broken a dating rule? "Do women still not eat when they go out with men?" she asked. "I remember that from high school, but I figured because we were older, it didn't matter."

"I'm glad you enjoyed your meal, and of course you're allowed to eat. Not enough women do."

Oh, great. "So your other women are superskinny?"

Steve paused in the act of pouring them each another glass of wine. "Okay, I sense several potentially dangerous pitfalls in that sentence. Number one, I don't have 'other women.'"

"That's not what I've heard," Carly said breezily. She could certainly feel the two glasses of wine she'd already had and was about to indulge in a third. *So* not like her, but then it felt fun to be someone else for the night.

"I've heard you're quite the ladies' man. I was even warned about you."

"Really? What was the warning?"

"That you'd probably try to seduce me, but not to expect a real relationship."

As soon as the words were out, she covered her mouth with her fingers.

"I did *not* say that," she mumbled.

Steve grinned. "I'm afraid you did. Interesting. I didn't realize I had such a reputation. I don't know if I should be flattered or insulted."

"Flattered," she said, dropping her hand back to her waist. "That's how it was meant."

"Why don't I believe you?"

"Not a clue." She did her best to look completely innocent. "So, why don't you tell me more about your summer trips to that village in Mexico? I think it's so great you take those teenage boys with you and then you all build housing for the poor."

"There's nothing more to tell. Let's stay on the subject of my seducing you."

"Not a good idea."

He looked at her as if trying to decide if he should pursue it or not. Carly crossed her fingers that he wouldn't. Right now she was a little drunk and very confused. She'd come into the dinner with clear-cut ideas about not being attracted to Steve, and now she found she was. The feelings were different from her wild, visceral reaction to Adam, but still intriguing. Jeez, who would have believed that less than three months after her divorce she would have thoughts about getting involved with two different guys?

Not that either had actually asked, but there were possibilities, and she liked that about them.

"I didn't realize you were such a lightweight," Steve said. "You're swaying in your seat after only two glasses of wine."

"Three," she said, pointing at the full glass in front of her.

"You haven't drunk that one yet, and I'm thinking you probably shouldn't. Who knows what would happen?"

She grinned.

He shook his head. "That does it. Less liquor for you."

"I would have thought you would like me drunk."

"I like to think I'm the kind of guy who can get his girl without help from alcohol." He flagged down the waiter and asked for the check.

"What about our walk on the beach?" she asked. "You said we were going to do that."

"I think we should save that for another time. I don't want you falling in."

"I'm not that drunk."

"You could have fooled me."

Carly didn't remember much about the drive home. She enjoyed her buzz and her newfound interest in Steve. When he parked in front of the B and B, she turned toward him in eager anticipation of his kiss. But instead of pulling her close and laying one on her, he lightly touched her cheek.

"Thanks for dinner," he said.

"That's my line. I had a nice time."

"Me, too. We'll have to do it again."

He smiled at her and got out of the car.

Carly blinked in confusion. That was it? He wasn't going to kiss her? Why? Hadn't he had a good time?

He opened the passenger door and she stepped out into the cool night.

"You didn't kiss me," she said before she could stop herself.

"I know," he said with a chuckle. "This is your first dating experience since the divorce. I thought I'd take it slow."

That was so nice, she thought happily. He was really nice. She liked nice. And him.

"Okay," she said. "It's not like I'm going anywhere."

"Good to know."

He walked her to the front door, lightly kissed her cheek, then opened the door and gave her a little push inside.

"I'll give you a call in a couple of days," he promised.

She waved her fingers at him and wondered if men calling when they said they would really happened these days, or if the male of the species was as undependable as she remembered.

She stepped into the empty parlor. The wine buzz had faded enough to make her rethink her question about him kissing her, and she was grateful that he'd held back. She didn't know what, if anything, could happen with Steve, but whatever it was wouldn't be helped by rushing. Far better to—

"How was your evening?"

She turned toward the voice and saw Adam sitting on the bottom stair.

The buzz returned, but it had nothing to do with wine and everything to do with the man.

Funny how it didn't matter that he was casually dressed or slightly rumpled or even too young. Just looking at him made her all soft and wet and wanting. As if she were melting from the inside out.

"Dinner was good," she said, trying not to stare, yet not able to look away.

"Steve, huh? So there *is* competition."

"Oh, there's not," she said before she could stop herself, then figured she might as well dig the hole deeper. "I mean I like Steve. He's a really great guy. But it's not the same."

Adam rose. "How is it different?"

"He's the kind of man women want to marry, and you're the kind of man women want..."

"Want? Want to what?"

She could get lost in his dark eyes. She heard the phrase a hundred times, read it a thousand, and it finally made sense. She wanted to lose herself in *him*, in what he could do and how he could make her feel.

"There's no 'to,'" she whispered. "That was the end of the sentence."

"Oh."

He moved closer, until she had to tilt her head back to meet his gaze.

"So you want me," he whispered, even as he bent down and pressed his lips to the side of her neck.

She'd planned to say no. She'd planned to tell him that she meant women in general, not her in particular. But instead she closed her eyes as she felt the warmth of his firm, yet soft mouth brush against her sensitized skin.

Shivers and tingles and goose bumps raced all over her body. A moan started low in her chest and gradually rose until she had no choice but to let it out. She swayed, reached out for something stable and encountered…him.

The second she put her hands on his shoulders, he surged forward and wrapped his arms around her. He pressed his mouth to hers in a demanding kiss that had her clinging to him even as she parted her lips and circled his tongue with hers.

Passion didn't begin to describe the need that exploded between them. One second there was rational thought, with her worries about her saggy breasts and dimpled thighs, the next nothing mattered but Adam and his touch. She didn't care about her appearance, or the fact that his last lover had probably been a twenty-two-year-old supermodel. She didn't think about appropriate or inappropriate or right or wrong.

"Come to my room," he murmured as he kissed his way along her jaw.

Carly felt too aroused to play hard to get. She had a brief thought that she couldn't remember the last time she'd shaved her legs, then she figured she couldn't worry about that now.

"Okay," she breathed.

He led her to the elevator. The short trip allowed them to hold on to each other, even as they kissed over and over. When the doors opened, she was conscious enough to make sure there weren't any other guests in the hallway before following him to his room.

Adam unlocked the door and motioned for her to precede him. When they were both inside, he turned on a lamp and turned off several complicated-looking pieces of equipment.

The video camera! He'd taped Jack and her mother moving furniture around.

"Are you—"

"All off," he said as he flipped the last switch.

She watched monitors, lights and displays go dark.

"But just so you don't worry." He walked to a long power strip and pulled the plug out of the wall.

His genuine concern made her smile, while the lingering effect of his kisses made her want him. She walked over and wrapped her arms around him.

"You're one of the good guys," she said.

"I try to be."

He cupped her face in his hands and began to kiss her again. Even as he slipped his tongue inside her mouth and made her squirm, he urged her backward. She went with the movement until she felt the bed behind her.

Before she could actually think about what was happening and get nervous, he dropped his hands to her waist and his mouth to her neck.

There was something to be said for a patient man, she thought, as he licked and nibbled his way down the V of her dress. Neil always acted as if the preliminaries were simply something he had to get through so that he could get off, but Adam took each step with enthusiasm. He moved slowly down her chest until he reached the curve of her breast, then he lightly kissed the sensitive flesh.

He shifted to her other breast, then moved higher and higher until she had to let her head fall back so he could nibble along the other side of her neck.

While his mouth kept her gasping and lost in sensation, his hands began a dance of their own. He stroked up and down her back before slipping down to her fanny. He cupped the curves and squeezed. She instinctively arched her hips forward, which brought her in contact with his body.

He was hard. She felt the thick ridge against her belly. Delight filled her.

"You want this," she said as she opened her eyes and looked at him.

He frowned. "Why wouldn't I?"

"Oh, give me a minute and I'll give you a hundred reasons."

"Carly, you're beautiful. You move with a sensual grace that leaves me weak. I love your face, your body, the feel of your skin."

Her heart stopped. No one had ever said anything like that to her before. Not even as a joke.

"Okay," she said breathlessly. "We can do it now."

He chuckled. "Not yet."

He kissed her. She let herself get lost in the pleasure of what he did to her. When he reached for the zipper on her dress, she silently urged him to go faster. When the garment fell to the ground and he cupped her breasts in his large hands, she gave a sigh of thanks.

He moved with the confidence of a man used to pleasing women. He circled her breasts, exploring them through her bra, nearing the nipples, but never touching them. Closer and closer until she finally grabbed his wrists and moved him into place.

His thumbs swept over the tight peaks. They both moaned. Heat made her ache and swell until she thought she couldn't wait another second.

"Adam," she breathed.

"Me, too."

He stepped back and reached for the hem of his T-shirt. While he peeled it off, she stepped out of her sandals, then sat on the edge of the bed to take in the show.

He was as beautiful without clothes as she'd imagined. Hard muscles made him look more like a perfect sculpture than a man, right up until he pulled off his boxers and his large erection jutted out toward her. That looked real enough.

In that moment, as she stared at his nakedness, she realized she'd only been with one other man. She'd gotten close with a few guys at college, but she'd been a virgin when she'd met Neil. There had only ever been that one penis in her life.

She reached out to touch Adam. He stood perfectly still as she brushed her fingers against the hard tip, then stroked the length of him. So smooth, she thought. Soft, soft skin surrounding hard desire.

He looked different than Neil had. About the same length, but thicker. The hair at the base was dark instead of red. She leaned in and licked the head of his arousal.

Different taste, she thought even as Adam sucked in a breath.

"You probably shouldn't do that again," he said in a strained voice. "I'd rather not lose it."

She laughed. "As if that's a danger."

He crouched down in front of her. "Don't say that. Don't even think it. I want to be with you. Believe that."

Before she could figure out what to say in response, let alone speak it, he stood and moved onto the bed, pulling her with him.

Then they were a tangle of arms and legs and his hands were everywhere. He unfastened her bra without looking.

Even as he slipped it off, he bent down and sucked on her nipples.

Fire raced through her in flames of need. She forgot to be unsure or embarrassed or even wonder if she'd been doing it wrong all these years. She held on and tried to catch her breath when he slipped off her panties and eased his fingers inside her.

Too much, she thought hazily. Too much felt too good. He explored all of her, pausing at the parts that made her gasp and cling and squirm. He rubbed faster and faster until the ground gave way and she flew into her orgasm.

It went on and on until she wondered if it would ever stop. Then he was kissing her and shifting. He grabbed a condom from the nightstand and slipped it on, even as he kept kissing her. Then he was inside and she felt herself tightening, pushing, reaching.

She came again. He pumped in and out of her, each thrust filling her with more pleasure. She wrapped her legs around his hips, urging him deeper. It was too good. It was incredible. She couldn't breathe, couldn't speak, couldn't do anything but feel him on top of her, in her.

At last he gave one hard pulse and stilled. Every muscle in his body tensed.

"Carly," he gasped as she felt his release. He stared at her and she would swear she could see into his soul.

* * *

It had been the best sex of her life. Okay, sure that was probably due to a long stretch of doing without and the thrill of a new partner. Or maybe it was turning forty and that sexual peak thing she was always reading about in magazines. Whatever the cause, she felt content and boneless.

"I have to get back to my own bed," she said after Adam had rolled off her and pulled her close. "Either my mother or my daughter finding me here would raise too many questions."

He kissed her shoulder. "I promise you that neither of them make regular appearances in my room."

"Good to know, but I still should be going."

The thing was, she didn't want to move. She wanted to make love again, this time more slowly. She wanted to feel those sensations again. She wanted him inside of her, claiming her with a mastery that made her feel both feminine and empowered.

He placed his hand on her breast and rubbed his fingers against her nipple.

"What about round two?" he asked.

There was a round two? She hadn't experienced that since the early days with Neil.

"I was thinking about it," she admitted, "but I wasn't sure you'd be able to, um, well..."

He leaned over and kissed her. "And if I can?"

He shifted slightly. Something very hard and promising poked her thigh.

"I can go back to my room later."

"That's my girl."

CHAPTER 14

Carly spent the next morning walking around trying not to grin like a fool. She was relaxed, refreshed and delightfully sore. Could life get any better?

Adam cornered her in the laundry room, where she was doing an inventory count on sheets. He came up behind her and grabbed her by the waist, turned her in his arms and kissed her senseless.

"Last night was incredible," he murmured. "When can we do it again?"

"What are you doing at midnight?" she asked.

He grinned. "Your room or mine?"

"We could try my bed this time. I think it's been a long time since it's seen any action."

"I'll be there." He kissed her again. "I told you I have to run into San Francisco, right? I'm meeting a guy from work for lunch. He thinks he's made a couple of important breakthroughs."

"You mentioned it, yes."

"Good. I don't want you thinking I'm bailing on you."

He was so earnest, she thought happily. As if her feelings mattered. Okay, this could never last, but she had a feeling it was going to be really good in the short term.

"You're sweet to worry about me. I'll be fine."

"I might be late. If we get to talking about solid fuels, who knows what could happen? But I'll be back by midnight."

She shivered in anticipation. "I'll be waiting."

"Good."

They kissed again before he left. As soon as he walked out of the laundry room, Carly counted to twenty before going up the stairs and calling for her mother.

"Let them know I'm on my way," she said. "I'm going to pick up Jack, then drive directly to the equipment rental."

She and Adam might have just done the wild thing an amazing three times in a single night, but that didn't mean she wasn't still going to try to convince him that the ghost was real. With Adam gone for several hours, she and Jack would put his electromagnet plan into action. With luck, that would do the trick.

* * *

No one had actually considered the dimension and weight of the magnet, Carly thought, as she and Jack wheeled the heavy cart onto the elevator.

She stepped back and stared at the device. "It looks like something out of a science fiction movie," she said. "Is this going to work?"

"It'll be great," Jack promised.

Tiffany hovered in the hall. "Should you guys ride up in the elevator with it? Won't that be too much weight?"

Carly looked at the metal device, the cart and the small elevator. "Good point. We'll take the stairs."

She leaned in, pushed the button for Adam's floor, then jumped back. Jack, Tiffany and she raced up the two flights, then hurried down the hall to meet the elevator when the doors slowly opened.

It was early afternoon and all their guests seemed to be out enjoying the sunny Saturday weather. Good thing, she thought as Jack slipped in behind the magnet and pushed. Carly and Tiffany grabbed the front of the cart and pulled. The large wheels began to slowly turn. If anyone saw them right now, they would run screaming for the hills.

"What is this supposed to do?" Tiffany asked.

"In theory, it will disrupt Adam's equipment and convince him there's been some kind of ghost dropping by," Carly said as she pulled with all her might.

The heavy cart finally rolled free of the elevator. She went around back to help Jack push as they urged it toward Adam's room.

"It's been two weeks, Mom. If he doesn't believe now, he's not going to."

"I'm not giving up," Carly said, between gasps as she pushed harder.

At last the cart was in place. Jack strung the thick power cord out a window and down to the portable generator that had been provided to run the magnet. He went downstairs and a few minutes later the entire house shook as he started the generator.

Tiffany raced to the window. "Ready?" she yelled. She turned to Carly. "He's giving me a thumbs-up. Go for it, Mom."

Carly flipped the switch on the jumbo magnet. For a second there was only a faint hum, then the afternoon exploded into a cacophony of thumps and crashes and screeches as throughout the house metal objects did their best to fly toward the magnet.

Carly swore under her breath. Obviously she hadn't thought this through. A particularly loud crash made her wince, but she left the magnet on for a full minute before turning it off.

Tiffany stared at her wide-eyed. "What just happened?"

"To be honest, I don't want to know."

The damage was mostly minor. Several metal cooking utensils and pans had flown out of open shelves and up to the ceiling, only to crash to the ground a minute later when the magnet was turned off. Serving trays had taken the same journey, as had all the paper clips in Carly's office. Her file cabinets had walked halfway across the floor. Drawers stood open. Her lamp was a casualty of attempted flight.

"It's so weird," Tiffany said when she ran into the office. "My bed is nearly out the door."

"Probably the metal frame. What about other stuff?"

"A few of my belts are on the floor. Jack says you need to check your computer disks. The floppies could be messed up."

Carly sank into her chair. "I don't want to know what the guest rooms look like. I sure hope this worked."

"We still have the locks to try," her daughter reminded her. "The automatic ones. They'll be fun."

Carly nodded, but she wasn't convinced. What if Adam didn't believe? What if she couldn't convince him?

* * *

"You're quiet," Adam said around one in the morning, when they'd finished making love and were simply trying to catch their breath.

"I was wondering how your day went. Did you have fun?"

Had he noticed that a giant magnet had gone off outside his room?

"It was good. I won't bore you with the technical details about what we discussed, but I think Will is on to something."

"Good."

He bent over her and kissed her. "Giant magnet, huh?"

She did her best not to show any emotion as she looked at him. "I have no idea what you're talking about."

"My equipment is all messed up and my floppies are trashed. Only one thing could have done that."

"A ghost?"

He chuckled. "No. A magnet. A really big one. How did you get it in the house?"

Her heart sank. Sure, the sex was good, but what did it matter in the face of her family's financial ruin?

"Why can't you just believe?" she asked as she sat up. "Ghosts are real."

"No, they're not. We both know that, Carly."

"I don't." She moved to the side of the bed and reached

for her clothes. "I don't know that for a second. You can tell me what your monitors say all you want. I don't care. I remember her. Mary is a part of my childhood. She was here, in this house. I've seen her and I don't care what anyone says. I believe, and if you don't, it changes everything."

He raised himself up on his elbow. "Is that the price of this relationship?"

"What relationship? You're here for another week, then you're leaving." She pulled on her panties, then grabbed her T-shirt. "How can you do this to me?"

"Do what?"

"Ruin me. If you go out and write your paper, or whatever it is you do, this B and B will lose over half our business. We'll never make it. My mom will sell. This house had been in our family nearly a hundred and fifty years. You don't have the right to take that away from us."

"I'm not. I'm simply telling the truth. I'm sorry about the house, but I don't believe you're going to lose it. You're stronger than you think."

She wasn't. She could feel herself getting weaker by the second.

"I've worked so hard and there's so much left to do." She pulled on her T-shirt, then grabbed his hands. "Adam, please. Don't do this."

"I care about you, Carly, but I won't lie."

"I'm not asking you to lie. I'm asking you to keep quiet."

"They're not that different."

"They are to me." She released him and turned away. "There's nothing I can say to change your mind?"

"No. I'm sorry. This isn't about you."

"Then who is it about?"

He didn't say anything for a long time. Finally she heard him get out of bed and pull on clothes. "You want me to go?"

"Yes."

She wasn't sure if he meant to leave her room or the B and B. Did it matter? Sure, she would miss him when he left, but she would miss the house more. To have come so far, only to lose everything now.

"I'm sorry," he said as he walked to the door. "I never meant to hurt you."

"Too bad. If that had been your plan, think of how successful you could feel right now."

She waited until he was gone, then she collapsed back on the bed and buried her face in a pillow. How could everything have gone so wrong so quickly? And how on earth did she make things right?

"Mom?"

Tiffany hovered outside Carly's office. Carly looked up

from her computer, where she'd been searching for small towns with good schools. If they had to move again, she wanted to make sure her daughter had a chance at a great education.

"What's up?" she asked, trying for cheerful and not sure she'd succeeded. The past two days had been one giant hurt that she'd tried to keep to herself.

"I don't know. You seem different. Are you okay?"

Carly smiled at her daughter. "I'm fine, but you know what I need?"

"What?"

"Some time away from here. Let's go into town and have ice cream for dinner."

"Really? Just the two of us?"

"Absolutely. Only don't tell Grandma."

"I won't. She'd totally freak."

Thirty minutes later they sat across from each other with two large chocolate sundaes between them.

"Bon appétit," Carly said.

Tiffany giggled and took a big bite. "This is great."

"I'm sure we'll both have stomachaches later, but it will be so worth it."

"You bet."

They ate in silence for a few minutes. Carly felt the first

stirrings of a sugar rush. Maybe it would be enough to get her mind off Adam.

He'd chosen not to leave the B and B, so she'd spent the past two days avoiding him. She'd canceled the order for the remote locks—they wouldn't fool him—and resigned herself to the demise of their status as a haunted house. After running the numbers without Mary as an enticement, she'd discovered what she already knew—no ghost meant no profits. It was well and truly over.

"Jack feels bad the magnet didn't work," Tiffany said. "But he had a good time helping."

"I'm glad. He's been great." She glanced at her daughter. "You guys have been together for a while now."

"Nearly two months." Tiffany ducked her head and blushed. "It's my longest relationship ever."

"You're growing up."

"Enough to car date?"

"Nope."

"Mo-om!"

Carly set down her spoon. "I know you think I make up these rules to make you unhappy, but it's not true. I love you and you're the most important person in my life. I want to do everything I can to keep you safe."

"But Jack would never hurt me."

"I think he cares about you a lot, but that doesn't mean he can't hurt you without trying. Boys are different."

Tiffany rolled her eyes. She leaned forward and lowered her voice. "We're in a *restaurant*, Mom. Don't you dare bring up sex now!"

"I'll whisper," Carly said softly. "But it is about sex. Because Jack cares about you, he wants things. Sexual things." The fact that he was sixteen meant he would want those things even if he didn't care, but she wasn't about to get into that.

"He hasn't tried anything."

"He hasn't had a chance. But if the two of you were alone, in a car or at someone's house, it would be so easy. You start out kissing and one thing leads to another. Eventually you're going to have to make those choices on your own. I know that. But not at fifteen. You're not ready, and neither am I."

"But this shouldn't be about you. What about my life?"

"I want you to have fun, but that doesn't mean you can do what you want. I love you too much not to have rules."

"Rules aren't good."

"They can be. They can save you. Tiffany, I would give my life for you. I'm also willing to have you hate me from now until you go off to college if that's what it takes. That's how much I want you to have a good life."

She thought she might have gotten through, but she wasn't sure. Especially when her daughter sighed and said, "I'm still mad about the belly button ring."

"Me, too."

"But everyone has one."

"Name me twenty girls at school who have one."

"Okay, not everyone."

Carly smiled. "Name me ten."

Tiffany sighed again, then grinned. "How about one?"

"You are *so* not getting a belly button ring on my watch."

"Fine. I'll put it on my to-do list for when I turn eighteen. I'm gonna be really busy that day."

"I'll bet you are."

Tiffany grinned. "Want to come with me and get one yourself?"

"We'll talk."

Carly walked into her bedroom that evening to find Adam sitting on her bed. She came to a stop, not sure if she should be happy, angry or simply order him out.

"I don't want it to be like this," he said before she could speak. "I hate that you're mad at me."

"Do you expect me to be happy with what you're going to do?"

"I expect you to understand." He stood and moved toward her. "Dammit, Carly, we have something special here. Are you going to let that go because of some fake ghost?"

He was furious. She could see the temper in his eyes.

"What are you talking about?" she asked.

"Us. What we could have together."

Was he insane? "There's no us. You've been really sweet to me, and I appreciate that, but Adam, you live in Virginia. I'm here. At least until I have to move. You're seven years younger than me."

He grabbed her arms. "Do you really think that matters?"

"Of course."

He swore again and released her. She couldn't believe he was so upset.

"I thought this was just about sex," she said. "I thought—"

"What?" His gaze narrowed. "That I didn't care? That this was all just an easy game for me? That you were one more notch in the bedpost?"

Honestly? "Yes."

"No!" He cupped her face in his hands and kissed her

with a desperation that made her knees go weak. "I care about you, Carly. More than I have cared about anyone in a long time. You're amazing. I want us to make this work."

What *us?* What *this?* She couldn't get her mind around the fact that he thought they had a future.

"For how long?" she asked. "At what point will you want someone younger and newer?"

"Why does it always have to be about age?"

"Because age matters. I'm forty. I have a fifteen-year-old daughter. You're going to want kids someday and I'm not interested in doing that again. I don't even know if I *could* get pregnant, but I can tell you I don't want to."

"I've never been that interested in kids."

Ha. Like she believed that. "You say that now, but you'll change your mind."

"So you won't have a relationship with me because of something that might happen in the future?"

There were other things, too, although she couldn't think of them now. Truthfully, she'd never allowed herself to consider a future with Adam. Sure he was great and pretty much everything she'd ever wanted in a man, but *so* not for her.

"I can't deal with any relationship right now," she told him. "I just got a divorce. I'm not looking to get involved."

"So this is just bad timing?"

"Some of it. Plus I know you think you're in the right on the ghost thing, but I don't want to be with someone so willing to ruin me."

His eyes darkened. "That's too bad because I can't be with someone who wants me to lie for her."

"I don't want you to lie," she began, then stopped. Wasn't not telling the truth as he saw it a lie of omission? "I guess I do."

"I won't."

"I know." Perhaps in time she could appreciate his honesty, but right now it was just too hard.

"I'm leaving in a few days. I don't want it to end like this."

"How do you want it to end?"

"With a promise for the future."

"I can't give you that. There's too much in my life right now. I don't know what's going on. If the B and B closes, I don't even know where Tiffany and I will live."

"Then come back to Virginia with me. I have a house. There's room."

She stepped back. "I've known you less than three weeks. I can't move in with you. Even if I wanted to, what kind of example does that set for my daughter? I'm having a hard enough time trying to keep her following the rules now."

"But I..." He reached for her. "I care about you."

She stepped back a second time. "Sometimes caring isn't enough."

"It has to be."

For the first time, she actually felt every one of the seven years that stretched between them and then some. He was so earnest and determined. As if he could will things to be the way he wanted.

She'd learned a long time ago that wanting had very little to do with anything.

"I'm sorry, Adam. It's not." She walked to her door and held it open.

He stared at her for a long time, then he shook his head and walked out into the hallway.

"You'll regret this," he said.

He might be right. There *was* something between them. There had been from the first second she'd seen him. But for now, her gut told her it was time to let him go.

The only good thing about feeling so crappy was that she didn't want to eat, Carly thought three days later as she sat at her desk and reached for her fifth cup of coffee. Maybe she could drop a couple of pounds and have to buy all new clothes because her old ones were hanging on her. It could happen.

Adam was leaving that afternoon and she had yet to speak with him. She hadn't—not since their last, very painful, encounter. She didn't know what to say.

She doubted he would want to know he was the best lover she'd ever had. Not only was that not much of a compliment, she had a feeling he wanted their time together to be about more than sex. And it was. She had feelings for him, but she didn't know what they were. Everything had happened too fast. She was too close to her divorce. He wanted the impossible, all the while planning to destroy her.

And she'd thought her life was complicated before.

She returned her attention to the spreadsheet in front of her. Once again she tried to make the numbers work without the ghost. If they could get enough business *before* word got out, maybe people would keep coming because they enjoyed the experience. Or if they could—

"I really like what you have done with the house. All those bookings. Isn't that lovely? I haven't seen the board so full in ages."

Carly froze in her seat. The voice was unfamiliar. Soft, female, British. Not sure she believed she'd heard it, terrified to turn around and see nothing, she could barely breathe.

"Have you seen Maribel? She's so round. In my day a woman was never allowed to show herself while she was in such a delicate condition. How things have changed. Carly? Are you all right?"

Carly swallowed, grabbed the arms of her chair and slowly turned to her left.

There, shimmering in the middle of the office, stood a slender young woman of twenty or so in a pale floor-length dress. Everything was the same, Carly thought in amazement. The way the fabric moved slightly, as if disturbed by a light breeze, the intricate braids in her hair, the glow, as if she were lit from within.

"M-Mary? Is that really you?"

"Of course." Mary turned from the bookings board and smiled. "I'm glad you're back. It wasn't the same around here after your father passed away. Oh, how rude. I never said I was sorry. I know how much you loved him. You must have been very sad."

Carly pushed to her feet. Her heart raced and her legs shook. Was this really happening? "I, ah, was. My mom's had a difficult time, as well. We… Where have you been?"

"Traveling." Mary pressed her lips together. "I don't mean

to speak out of turn, but your mother can be difficult. Always dithering."

"Okay. You're real, right? You're really here?"

"Of course I'm here. You've known me all your life. Why would you question my presence?"

"I just… You were gone for so long and my mother told me you never existed. That what I remembered were just stories I'd heard or made up."

Mary sniffed. "No imagination. That's why I never appeared to her."

Carly laughed. "Are you staying? I have had so many people asking about you."

Mary folded her hands together at her waist. "That depends. How are things here these days?"

"What? Oh, I'm taking over. My mother is going to retire to Las Vegas in a few years. That's in Nevada."

"I know. I've visited a few times. Interesting place. Well, if you'll be here, I would very much like to stay. Travel is so tiring at my age."

"I would imagine."

Her mind whirled. This was real. Mary had returned. The house had a ghost. Carly wanted to dance with delight, she wanted to scream and cry and she didn't know what. But she also didn't want to upset Mary by "dithering."

"There's been an interesting development while you've been gone," she said, trying to stay calm. "A gentleman is staying here. Adam Covell. He doesn't believe in ghosts. In fact his purpose is to discredit the B and B. He's going to write a paper. I've been trying to convince him you're real, but it hasn't worked."

"How intriguing. Tell me about this man. Is he young?"

"Younger than me. Very handsome."

"You smile when you say that. Is he of some import to you?"

"I don't know. I like him a lot, but… It's confusing."

"Men generally are." Mary smiled. "Have you been intimate with him?" She held up a slender, glowing hand. "I know, I presume with that question. You have every right to refuse to answer, but I hope you will not."

Carly grinned. "Oh, yeah. We've been intimate."

"How lovely." Mary's smiled widened. "I was married for a time, before my demise. At first the intimacies of the marriage bed were quite distasteful, but after a time…" She paused and delicately cleared her throat. "I will only say that I did not turn my husband away."

You go, girl, Carly thought. "He's leaving in the afternoon. Can you help me convince him you're real?"

"It will be my pleasure."

CHAPTER 15

Carly took the elevator to Adam's floor. Mary would, of course, make her own way there.

She was real, Carly thought with equal parts delight and amazement. She hadn't made it all up. Mary was still very much a part of her past.

She'd already thought about several things they could do together and she very much wanted her friend to meet Tiffany. Talk about an interesting relationship if the two of them hit it off.

Still smiling at the thought of the nearly two hundred-year-old ghost and her fifteen-year-old chatting about boys and fashion, she stopped in front of Adam's door and knocked.

He opened it at once and when she saw him, she was stunned by the dark circles under his eyes.

"What's wrong?" she asked.

"What the hell do you think?"

She wanted to believe he was upset at the thought of leaving her, but that didn't make sense, did it?

Without saying anything, he grabbed her arm, pulled her inside, shut the door behind her and kissed her.

She felt herself responding to his touching, wanting him with more passion than was humanly possible to contain. She tried to get closer, to make his need and her need meld.

"How can you say there's nothing between us?" he asked bitterly as he stepped back.

"I guess I can't."

"What?" He stared at her.

"I have feelings for you," she said slowly. "I just don't know what they are."

He growled and pulled her close again. "You're damned annoying. Do you know that?"

"I'm aware it might be a possibility. But before we get into this, I have someone I want you to meet."

She moved away and turned to see Mary standing in the room. The ghost looked amused.

"Am I interrupting?" she asked politely.

"Not really. Adam, this is Mary."

Carly waited for his shriek or gasp or something. Instead

he picked up a shirt he'd already folded and tucked it into the open suitcase on the bed.

"Nice to meet you."

Carly stared at him. "Adam, she's a ghost."

He didn't bother looking up. "Nice trick with the lights. How are you doing it?"

"I'm not doing anything. She's really a ghost. This is Mary. I told you about her. She's been traveling and now she's back."

He glanced at the shimmering presence again and shrugged. "I like the detail with the costume."

Mary frowned. "I am not wearing a costume, Mr. Covell."

"Uh-huh."

Carly wanted to stamp her foot like a two-year-old. How could Adam not believe?

"It's all right," Mary said soothingly. "Mr. Covell, if I may have your attention for a moment?"

Adam glanced up as Mary glided through the wall, then returned.

"Hologram," he said, sounding particularly unimpressed.

Mary nodded, then levitated a chair and turned it slowly in the air.

"I saw that when I was eight and my parents took me to Disney World."

"I've been there," Mary said as she lowered the chair. "Lovely, lovely place. All those happy children." She turned her attention to Adam. "You, sir, are most difficult."

"Thanks."

"He thinks he's really smart," Carly said.

Adam smiled. "I *am* really smart."

Carly ignored that and pointed at his equipment. Various lights were blinking and several gauges seemed to be vibrating.

"Doesn't that mean anything?" she asked.

"Nope. I have to get everything recalibrated when I get home. Your magnet really screwed it all up."

Oh, wasn't that just perfect!

"Mary, you have to think of something. If Adam doesn't believe in you, my mother is going to have to sell this place."

Mary sighed. "Not more new owners. It took me nearly fifty years to adjust to your family." She eyed Adam. "Very well. Although I do protest having to go to this length. It is very disconcerting and far too great an intimacy when we have such a short acquaintance."

She seemed to draw herself up to her full height, then she glided purposefully to Adam. He watched with interest, but didn't seem the least bit afraid. Not even when she slipped right inside him.

Carly gasped. What on earth?

At first nothing happened. Then Adam stiffened, went completely white and swore. Mary left him as smoothly as she'd entered. She paused in the center of the room and stared at him.

"I trust you are now more inclined to believe I exist."

Adam staggered a few steps, then sank onto the edge of the bed.

"Holy Mother of God," he breathed. "What the hell just happened?"

Carly rushed over and sat next to him. "Mary sort of merged with you. Are you all right?"

"He is perfectly fine," Mary told her. "Just a little muddled by the experience." She raised her eyebrows. "He's very fond of you. Were you aware?"

Adam shook his head, then turned to Carly and grabbed her by the shoulders. "She's a ghost."

Carly grinned. "I believe I mentioned that earlier."

"No. A ghost. A real ghost. We connected. I know her history, her thoughts. I know about her family." He stared at Mary. "You're real."

"For someone with as much education as you have, sir, you're not very bright, are you?" She shook her head. "My work here is complete. Good day."

She glided through the wall and disappeared.

* * *

"I don't want to leave," Adam said as he loaded his equipment into his SUV.

"Mary isn't going anywhere," Carly reminded him. "She's promised to make an appearance from time to time, just to keep the guests on their toes. I think she's looking forward to it."

"I still can't believe she's real."

"Having your body momentarily inhabited by a spectral phenomenon is enough to convince even the staunchest cynic?"

"Absolutely." He pulled her close and kissed her. "But I was talking about not wanting to leave you."

Carly didn't know what to do with that information. "Adam," she began, before he cut her off with a quick kiss.

"Stop. I know exactly what you're going to say and I don't want to hear it. I'll be back to convince you in a couple of months."

"You don't have to do that."

"I want to."

She had to admit his intensity was appealing. While she wasn't sure what she wanted from the future, having Adam around wouldn't be so bad.

"Just so we're clear, I'm not interested in getting married again," she told him.

He grinned. "You say that now, but I'll change your mind."

"I don't think so." She was more interested in sex than something permanent.

"Don't go falling for any math teachers while I'm gone."

"You don't have to worry about that."

"But you'll be dating him."

"Occasionally." Steve had called and asked her out for Friday.

Adam shook his head. "That guy's too old for you."

He kissed her again, then climbed into the SUV. After opening the window, he leaned out.

"I'm coming back," he promised.

"You know where to find me."

Carly hung up with the reporter and grinned. Ever since Adam's article on the house and Mary had been posted on the national registry Web site and had been picked up by several newspapers, she'd been flooded with calls. Everyone wanted to hear the story and then come stay for the night. They were booked solid every night through the summer and every weekend through the first of the year.

"Not bad," Carly said aloud as she added the reporter's

name to the growing wait list. He'd wanted to bring his wife up for their seventh anniversary.

The phone rang again. If this kept up, she was going to have to get a full-time assistant.

"Chatsworth-by-the-Sea, may I help you?"

"I need to speak with Carly Spencer," a woman said.

"This is Carly."

"Oh, hi. I'm Annie Carter. My daughter is in school with your daughter. I was calling to find out what you knew about the party last Friday night."

"Party? I don't know about a party. Tiffany spent the night at a friend's house."

"Jessica something?"

Carly got a bad feeling in her stomach. "That's right. But I called and spoke with Jessica's mother."

Annie sighed. "So did I. Unfortunately the person we spoke with was Jessica's older sister who thought this was all pretty funny. There was a huge party at the house. It lasted until all hours and there were boys there. Some from college."

The bad feeling doubled in size and Carly got very, very angry.

"I appreciate you telling me, Annie."

The other woman chuckled. "Okay. I tell by the tone of your voice that you're pissed, too."

"More than pissed."

"I can't believe my daughter lied to me."

"Right back at you," Carly said. "Tiffany is in for some serious grounding."

"I hear you. I just wanted to let you know about the party. I have a couple of other parents to call. Oh, doesn't your daughter know a boy named Jack?"

"Yes. They're friends—semi-boyfriend and girlfriend."

"He was there, too."

Carly's anger grew until it threatened to explode. It nearly doubled in size. She said goodbye, hung up and threw a pen at the wall for good measure.

She couldn't believe it. How could Tiffany have done this to her? She'd thought things were better between them. Obviously she'd been seriously wrong.

She stood and stalked out of the office, only to run into her mother. "Have you seen Tiffany?" Carly asked her.

"She's upstairs in her room. She said she had a lot of homework and wanted to get it finished bfore dinner." Rhonda smiled. "I think our little girl is finally growing up and learning to be responsible."

"Oh, I think our little girl is terrified I'm going to find

out about her Friday-night activities and wants to make sure she doesn't get in too much trouble by being a sweetie now."

"What happened?"

"Tiffany lied about spending the night at a friend's, and instead went to a boy-girl party that lasted until who knows when. Plus, her girlfriend's older sister played mom when I called to confirm there would be adult supervision."

"Then she's going to be in big trouble," Rhonda told her.

"Oh, yeah. I'm going to talk to Tiffany."

Rhonda nodded. "I'll take care of the appetizers and wine."

Carly glanced at the clock. It was nearly four. "Thanks, mom. I appreciate the help. You're the best."

Rhonda looked faintly surprised, then smiled and left for the kitchen. Carly took the elevator to the third floor, then climbed the tower stairs. She knocked once on Tiffany's door, then entered.

Her daughter sat at her desk, hard at work on her homework.

"Hi, Mom," she said cheerfully. "I'm nearly done here. Want me to help with the appetizers when I'm finished?"

If only this pleasant, happy child was really her daughter. But alas…

"I just received a call from a parent of one of the girls at your school. Apparently there was no sleepover Friday night. There was a boy-girl party. You went with Jack." Carly felt her temper flare again. "You lied, Tiffany. You flat-out lied. Then Jessica's older sister pretended to be her mother to fake me out."

Tiffany stared at her. Utter shock widened her eyes. "What? No. That's not..."

Carly held up a hand. "Don't make the mistake of lying to me a second time. That will only make things worse."

Her daughter pressed her lips together, then pushed to her feet.

"But it's not fair. How did anyone find out? We all swore we weren't going to say anything. Who blabbed?"

"I haven't a clue. But here's the thing. You can kiss your sleepover privileges goodbye. You're grounded for the next month. You will lose phone privileges and you won't be seeing Jack."

"What?"

"He was there, too. I expected better of the two of you." Oddly enough, she was almost more disappointed in Jack than Tiffany. She expected her daughter to try to get away with things, but she'd thought he was different. Which was silly. He was sixteen. Just because he didn't screw up in front of her didn't mean he wasn't a regular kid.

"But I have to see Jack."

"No, you don't."

"This is so unfair."

"There's more to your grounding, but I haven't figured out what it's going to be," Carly said, keeping her voice calm. "You chose to lie, you chose to mislead me and you chose to break the rules. You made every bit of this happen and now you're going to face the consequences."

"I hate you!" Tiffany screamed.

"I'm sure you do." She unplugged the phone that had only been recently restored from the last grounding. After collecting Tiffany's cell phone from the nightstand, she turned to leave.

"Just so we're clear, I'm calling Jack's mother to tell her about the party."

"What? You can't. This is too embarrassing."

"Should have thought about that before. Consider yourself stuck on the property here until the second week of July. I suppose you can leave to see your dad, but that's it."

"You can't do that. It's nearly summer vacation."

"Huh. You're right. You should have thought about that before."

Carly stepped out into the hallway. Something hard slammed into the door, but it didn't phase her in the least.

For once she didn't mind that her daughter was upset with her. Tiffany had screwed up and now she would face the consequences. It was time to make sure there was only one professional victim in the house.

"I don't like these people one bit," Rhonda said as she peered out the kitchen window. "The way they dress, and their music. They'll probably murder us in our beds."

"I think they'll be more creative than that," Carly said. She poured herself a second cup of coffee. "They're horror writers, Mom. They're fine."

Her mother sniffed loudly. "They're odd."

"I know, and I'm okay with that."

Funny how she was. Tiffany hadn't spoken to her in nearly three days and she had a feeling Jack was pissed at her, as well, but that was all right, too.

"Neil's here," Rhonda said. "What do you suppose he's going to do with Tiffany this time?"

"I haven't a clue." Carly carried her coffee out to the front porch and waited for her ex-husband.

When he strolled up the steps, she smiled. "Hi. Tiffany's in a bad mood because she's grounded for a month." She told him about the party. "I'm sure you think I'm being too tough, but I would appreciate your support by not telling her that. Also, please don't take her shopping this weekend. She's still grounded."

Neil nodded. "I know, I know. No belly button rings, no late nights, no inappropriate movies. Jeez, Carly, don't you ever get tired of being an adult?"

"Sometimes, but it's too late to go back."

"Not necessarily. My boat's nearly ready to go. You could leave all this and sail with me to Hawaii."

"What?" He couldn't be serious.

He shuffled his feet. "It could be fun. Like it was before."

"Before when?"

"You know. Back when things were good between us."

Before she had grown up, she would bet. "Thanks for asking, but I'd rather stay right here."

He frowned. "Why?"

She leaned against the front of the porch. The railing would need painting again soon. There was a broken washer, a full house and the produce delivery was late. Maribel had gone on maternity leave and her daughter freaked out every single morning before she started baking. Carly knew it would be a long two months until her friend returned to work. And it was summer—their busiest time.

She seemed to go from crisis to crisis. But wasn't that life?

A day-to-day world where very little was in her control? And isn't that what made it wonderful?

She might have come here because she'd had nowhere else to go, but she was staying for far better reasons.

"I like my life, Neil. I don't want to run away."

And if she did, it wouldn't be with him.

"What is there to like?" he asked, obviously genuinely baffled by her statement.

She thought for a second, then grinned. "Everything."

Read on for another exciting NEXT novel that will have all your friends talking.

Here's an exciting sneak peak at Jennifer Archer's
SANDWICHED, *available now,*
from Harlequin NEXT.

I settle into a wicker chair, flip through the mail again, then place all but one piece on the patio table. The evening is cool but not uncomfortable. It's already dark out, but I don't care; I'm numb and blind to everything except the texture of the expensive envelope beneath my fingertips and the return address in the upper left corner. Gosset, Dusseldorf and Klein.

Shooing away a fly, I turn the envelope over to open it, but can't bring myself to lift the flap. "This is it, Max," I say, eliciting a tiny moan from the dog. He stops munching and trots over. "The end of life as I knew it. No more Bert. Hurray!" My throat tightens. Erin might as well be gone, too. From now on, it'll just be Mother and me.

It won't be so bad, I tell myself. Who needs men anyway? Who can trust 'em? I'll learn to knit. That's something Mother and I can do together. Night after night. In front of the television. *Wheel of Fortune*. Mother will cook delicious meals for me. What better way to fill the emptiness than with smothered steak and buttermilk biscuits. Blackberry cobbler? She might even make my favorite chocolate éclairs. I'll gain so much weight that I'll have to buy my clothing at the tent and awning store. Which won't be an issue anymore since I won't be trying to impress a man. Think how comfy I'll be. How content. Fat and happy.

And alone. With Mother.

Max yelps. I look down at him. He tilts his head to one side. His brown eyes appear sympathetic.

"I'm sorry, Max." I sniff. "It won't be just Mother and me. I'll have you, too. Since Dad's gone, you're the only male in my life worth bothering with, anyway. At least you don't leave dirty underwear on the bedroom floor."

With one final scratch to Max's head, I return my focus to the envelope. I open it, pull the paperwork out, unfold it, then set it aside, facedown. Why not see what else came in the mail and put off the inevitable? I make my way through bills, flyers, an invitation to a party to celebrate an associate's twenty-fifth wedding anniversary. Good for her. Thanks for rubbing it in. I reach for an envelope from Erin's school. The letter inside is for parents of seniors. A meeting's planned next week to discuss graduation plans: announcements, caps and gowns, the class party. Already.

A wave of sadness sweeps over me.

Erin. She's not a little girl anymore. But she's not as grown up as she thinks she is, either. She's pulling away from me, but still requires my guidance. More than ever. But I need a different approach now that she's older.

With a sigh, I return to the legal papers. Can't put them off forever. Maybe I've been looking at this divorce all wrong. Maybe it's a new beginning rather than an ending. A chance to discover new interests. To rediscover old ones. To do something for *me*, for a change. I should redefine my relationship with Erin, focus more on my career, spend more time with Mother. Can't all that be enough?

When I flip to the last page, Bert's signature jumps out at me. Then mine. I suck in a breath of cool air.

My tears taste salty and bittersweet as I stare at the document that ends my old life and launches a new one.

New and improved.

Here's an exciting preview of Mary Schramski's WHAT TO KEEP, available this August from Harlequin NEXT.

Greensville, NC
September 2000

I could tell you a story about how my uncle Grey Alexander left me Magnolia Hall because I was his favorite niece. Then you might think I visited him every summer to attend reunions, and our family was close and very loving. That's when I'd explain that Uncle Grey always sent me beautiful birthday cards, telephoned me on Christmas morning to wish me a happy, peaceful holiday. And at the end of our conversation he'd go on and on about how he wished I were home instead of in dusty Las Vegas.

I'd also tell you on the day he died I found out he made sure I, Juliette Carlton, a forty-year-old, three-time, divorced blackjack dealer, his beloved niece and misplaced Southern belle, inherited all he had, including the memories of a loving Southern family.

But none of it would be true.

Someone once told me the reason people lie is because it sounds better. They were right. And life, as my mother used to remind me over and over, is raw and ugly. Part of that is true. Life is raw and ugly if a person makes it that way. Maybe that's why my mother lied so much.

I've decided not to fabricate anything, especially to myself. At one time I was big on that. I'd tell myself I was happy when I wasn't, tell myself a man cared when he didn't.

So the truth is I inherited an old Southern house from a man who just happened to be my uncle. I barely had a few faded memories of him. I became the owner of his house because I'm the only family member left. And that one little mistake of Grey Alexander not making a will changed my life forever. Because before all this happened I believed money would make my life better, different, worth living. What I didn't know was that no amount of money could help me. It took something so strange, like inheriting an old Southern mansion that really didn't belong to me, to make me see what's really important.

The things to give away. And what to keep.